10. Can you live without a boy?

Anna and I just love doing the quizzes in magazines.

"What's it about?" I asked, finishing off my strawberry smoothie.

"Um." Anna folded the magazine pages back on each other. "It's called 'You and Your Lad: Suit Him or Boot Him?'"

"Er, you mean it's about boyfriends?"

"Der!" Anna grinned at me. "And isn't it great? This is the first time we've been able to answer one of these girlfriend/boyfriend quizzes properly."

"What do you mean, 'properly'?" I wanted to know.

"You know," Anna explained. "It's the first time that we've had boyfriends. So we know what the *real* answers are rather than what we hope the answers would be if we had one."

I thought about what Anna said about knowing the real answers because we had boyfriends. I knew that was what she meant—and that was the bit I wasn't sure I liked.

Also available from Simon Pulse

Ella Mental: Life, Love, & More Good Sense
by Amber Deckers

All Mates Together
by Cathy Hopkins

Before Midnight
by Cameron Dokey

My Cup Runneth Over
by Cherry Whytock

Dancing Queen
by Erin Downing

10 Ways to Cope with Boys

Caroline Plaisted

SIMON PULSE

New York London Toronto Sydney

This book is a work of fiction. Any references to historical events, real people, or real locales are used fictitiously. Other names, characters, places, and incidents are the product of the author's imagination, and any resemblance to actual events or locales or persons, living or dead, is entirely coincidental.

SIMON PULSE

An imprint of Simon & Schuster Children's Publishing Division
1230 Avenue of the Americas, New York, NY 10020
Copyright © 2007 by Caroline Plaisted
Originally published in Great Britain in 2006 by Simon & Schuster UK Ltd., a CBS company
Published by arrangement with Simon & Schuster UK Ltd.
First U.S. edition 2007
All rights reserved, including the right of reproduction in whole or in part in any form.
SIMON PULSE and colophon are registered trademarks of Simon & Schuster, Inc.
Designed by Paula Russell Szafranski
The text of this book was set in Granjon.
Manufactured in the United States of America
First Simon Pulse edition January 2007
10 9 8 7 6 5 4 3 2 1
Library of Congress Control Number 2006928452
ISBN-13: 978-1-4169-3476-9
ISBN-10: 1-4169-3476-6

Chapter One

How Often Does He Text You?

Sometimes I really hate Sunday afternoons. They can be so boring. Your mum and dad nag you ("Have you done your homework? Are you sure?" "Are your shoes polished and ready for Monday?" "Are you really sixteen and no longer a baby?") and, even worse, if you've got a job on Saturday, you usually do have some coursework to finish.

And that's another thing—work. I quite like my job in loads of ways. I mean, there's the cash for a start. And the fact that I have a whole day without my disgusting baby brother, Jack, being irritating beneath my nose. Plus I don't get babyfied by my mum and dad trying to organize me. Mum especially. But—BIG but—I can't pretend that stacking shelves with breakfast cereals is exactly exciting. Or the getting-up-early-on-a-Saturday bit, either.

This particular Sunday afternoon, I was at my best mate Anna's house. Anna is just brilliant and we've been best friends for years. But I have to be honest, I'd actually gone round to Anna's to see Joey, her brother. Not her.

You see, Joey and I are going out with each other. Joey is just lush: He's dead good-looking, with white-blond hair, he wears cool clothes, he's fit, plays footie and cricket—and he's been going out with me for the last three months, since just after my six-teenth birthday.

Of course, I've known Anna forever, so I've known Joey for eons too. But he was never anything more than Anna's brother until the last year or so. You see, it was then that I realized he was so cute. So gorgeous. So perfect to be my boyfriend.

So anyway, when I saw Joey yesterday (we went to some party at one of Joey's friend's friend's), he said, "See you tomorrow, eh?" Now, I know he plays footie on Sunday mornings at the park, so I figured that if I went round to Anna's after lunch, he'd be there, back from the game.

The problem was, when I got round to Anna's,

Joey hadn't come back from football. Anna said she hadn't a clue where Joey was and why didn't I text him to find out? She seemed a bit surprised I hadn't already. Anyway, so then I did, but it was ages before he texted back and then, when he did, he just said @ Kevs.

"He's still at Kev's," I sighed.

"Good, that means I can still have you to myself!" Anna said. "Come on upstairs."

So we ended up in Anna's room, drinking a smoothie that she'd just made us with the new smoothie machine that Anna's dad had given her mum for her birthday.

"Hey—this one's not bad. In fact, it's quite good," I said, taking a sip from my glass.

"Don't worry—I wasn't going to make the egg-and-bacon mistake again," Anna giggled, remembering the most disgusting smoothie that she had made from a recipe in one of her mum's magazines for a breakfast smoothie. The idea was that you cooked the egg and bacon the night before and then swizzed it in the smoothie maker for breakfast the next morning. Eeew!

"I should hope not," I said, almost gagging on the thought of it. "It was like snot in a glass. That all went down in one gloop."

"Enough," Anna giggled.

"Gross," I laughed, putting my hand over my mouth at the thought of it. It had even smelled disgusting.

I was slumped back on a bean bag and leaned forward to grab a magazine from Anna's pile. It was the latest copy of *Get It!* and I hadn't seen it yet.

"Hey—there're some fabby jeans in there. Look ..." Anna jumped down from her bed, grabbed the mag, and started to flip through the pages.

"Thanks, I was looking at that!" I said.

"Trust me, Beth," Anna said, brushing my hand away as I tried to grab the magazine back. "There!"

"Sweet!"

She was right—the jeans were gorgeous. And they were also over one hundred pounds!

"Have you seen the price?" I squealed. "How can jeans be that much? Jeans that *I* want to have."

"They can if they are simply megagorgeous. I can't help it if I have expensive taste!" She smirked. "Aren't they just to die for, though?"

"They are," I agreed, and sighed as I thought of the pair that my mum had recently brought back from the market for me. They were labeled D&D and my mum thought that if I wore them everyone would think that I had a pair of Dolce and Gabbanas on. As if. My mother is *so* sad.

"I suppose Frankie will probably have a pair of those," Anna said.

Frankie is this desperate girl at school. She does modeling. Okay, she *is* a model. But only during the holidays—although she goes on and on and on about it. Puke, puke.

"Of course," I replied sarcastically. "She was probably given them as a present by the designer because she has the only bottom in the country worthy enough for them."

"Meeee-*ow*!" Anna laughed. "Except, of course, that her contract with New Look probably doesn't let her wear anyone else's jeans."

"Oh, with her contract, of course!"

And we giggled some more. You see, Frankie had told everyone who stood still longer than half a second about her brilliant career as a model as if she only ever modeled designer labels for *Vogue*.

The thing was, though, Anna and I had found La Frankie modeling in a magazine all right—only it was just T-shirts and shorts in the New Look catalog.

"I can still remember the look on her face when you told her about the catalog," I spluttered.

"She was *soo* cross," Anna sniggered. "It was fantastic."

It was true. Because we had hardly been able to

contain ourselves until we'd got back to school, taking the catalog with us to show everyone. Frankie was so pissed off with us when she walked in and realized that we'd all seen her in a bog-standard T-shirt rather than a Versace one.

"But I'm on an exclusive contract with New Look," Frankie had said, as if she was Kate Moss. As if New Look couldn't sell T-shirts without her in them. Please.

"Must be great to have an exclusive modeling contract," Anna said, back in her bedroom, back in the here and now.

"With New Look," I added, and we giggled helplessly some more.

Okay, okay. I appreciate that you might be thinking that Anna and I are being mean here. But you've got to know Frankie to really realize why she makes us feel like running away screaming every time she comes near. If I told you that she'd got this patronizing, sort of whiny voice, you'd probably think, *Well—so what's the big deal in that?*

And there wouldn't be a big deal if that were the only freako thing about her. But if I then told you that she once blabbed on me and Anna when we'd persuaded our form tutor that we'd been given permission to have our study period sitting on the grass outside—I mean the *whole* class had to stay in because of her—then you might begin to realize the kind of person Frankie is. But she doesn't always do rotten things that are so obvious. That's kind of why she's quite so creepy. So sneaky. With her snidey little comments like "I didn't know they made kitten heels for feet *that* big" and "How clever of you to find your best jeans in a supermarket/charity shop."

And there was the time she let me walk out of the girls' loo and down the corridor into the assembly, in front of everyone, even though my skirt was tucked into my knickers. I mean, the *whole* school saw me! So maybe that explains a bit more why Frankie isn't exactly our favorite person.

Anyway, we carried on flipping through *Get It!*, drooling over the makeup, gasping at the "true life" stories (are they *really* for real?), and dribbling at some of the boys.

"Oh, here we go," Anna said, plonking the magazine down firmly on the floor and grabbing a pen from her desk. "It's quiz time!"

Anna and I just love doing the quizzes in magazines. You know, the ones where you have a question and a choice of three or four answers? Course, you can usually work out which ones to choose (and therefore lie through your teeth) to get the end result you want—so that you can end up as dead glamorous rather than a sag bag, or destined for pop stardom rather than karaoke crumble. Well, like I said, Anna and I love those quizzes and we both sat up, ready to answer those questions.

"What's it about?" I asked, finishing off my strawberry smoothie.

"Um." Anna folded the magazine pages back on each other. "It's called 'You and Your Lad: Suit Him or Boot Him?'"

I'd been thinking it would be about "You and Your Style" or maybe "You and Your Best Mate."

"Er, you mean it's about boyfriends?"

"Der!" Anna grinned at me. "And isn't it great? This is the first time we've been able to answer one of these girlfriend/boyfriend quizzes properly."

"What do you mean, 'properly'?" I wanted to know.

"You know," Anna explained. "It's the first time that we've had boyfriends. So we know what the *real* answers are rather than what we hope the answers would be if we had one."

You see, Anna was going out with Sam, one of Joey's best mates. They'd started to go out around about the same time that Joey asked me out the first time. Sam was tall and broad, manic about football—maybe even more than Joey was—in fact, seriously into sport full stop. Not only were Joey and Sam mates, they went to the same college, played on the same footie team, and were pretty inseparable. Except, that is, that Sam seemed to spend an awful lot more time with Anna than Joey did with me.

I thought back to what Anna said about knowing the real answers because we had boyfriends. I knew that was what she meant—and that was the bit I wasn't sure I liked. Because I wasn't certain that I wanted to reveal much about my boyfriend. Not to his *sister*, if you know what I mean. And we could usually make up the answers to the questions, but it sounded like Anna was taking this one pretty seriously.

"Okay then," I said. "Let's have a look."

Anna opened up the magazine again and put it down on the floor in front of us. We started our official quiz ritual, which meant reading all the questions, then going back and picking the right answers, rather than telling the truth (no one does that, surely?) and comparing our scores at the end. But it was looking like Anna wasn't planning on playing our usual game with this quiz. With great dramatic relish, she read all the questions aloud.

You and Your Lad: Suit Him or Boot Him?

1. How often does he text you?
a) At least ten texts a day
b) A couple of times a day
c) Once a day
d) A few times a week

"Blimey," I gasped. "Ten texts a day? Sounds a bit desperate, doesn't it?"

"Shut up and listen, will you?" Anna groaned. "As I was saying . . ."

2. How often do you see him?
a) Every day
b) About five times a week
c) On weekends only
d) It depends

"What's that got to do with anything?" I wanted to know. "What if your boyfriend's in Canada? You can't see him every day then, can you?"

"Er, no, obviously," Anna said with a puzzled, slightly impatient look on her face. "But I kind of guess this quiz assumes most teenage girls don't have many boyfriends in Canada. Can't you just chill?"

I shut my mouth, feeling embarrassed.

"Thank you. . . ."

3. Does he have a nickname for you?
a) Yes
b) Only in private
c) When he's feeling romantic
d) No

Anna looked at me, one eyebrow raised, daring me to say something.

Thank God Joey doesn't call me something like "Bunny," I thought. In fact, the idea of Joey calling me "Bunny" was making me giggle. Anna frowned at me and carried on.

4. What's your idea of a perfect date?
a) Snuggling up in the back seat of the cinema
b) A candlelit dinner for two in a restaurant
c) Watching football on the telly
d) A double date with your best friend and her lad

Like I'd been on enough dates to know? Joey and I don't really "do" dates. Hmm, this was going to be tricky.

5. What's <u>his</u> idea of a perfect date?

a) Snuggling up in the back seat of the cinema

b) A candlelit dinner for two somewhere expensive—and he's paying

c) Watching football from the side of the pitch

d) Watching football on the telly

How was I supposed to know what went on in Joey's mind? Did Anna know what Sam was thinking?

Anna's face wasn't giving anything away as she continued reading the questions. Perhaps she was as baffled by the boys' brains as I was.

6. Is he a grown-up or a groan-up?

a) His favorite thing is a whoopee cushion

b) His favorite thing is his MP3 player

c) His favorite thing is his dog

d) His favorite thing is his teddy bear

"Supposing he's got all those things?" Anna asked me. I was tempted to ask why she was allowed to speak and I wasn't, but I was too interested in finding out what she was getting at.

"You mean Sam's got a teddy bear? And he's actually told you he has?" I said, my eyes agog that the megatall, megawide Sam has something as cute as a teddy.

"What's wrong with that?" Anna wanted to know.

"Er, nothing," I replied. "I mean—it's cute! Has Joey got a teddy?" If she said yes, maybe I could find out a bit more about Joey's cute side.

"You think I would go into Joey's room to find out? Gross!" Anna said, scrunching up her face in disgust.

7. Is your boyfriend your best friend?

a) You could tell him your darkest secret and he'd keep it

b) He's always ready to hug you when you cry

c) He spends as much time with the lads as with you

d) You'd never tell him when you were fed up about something

Anna was my best friend—so how could Joey be my best friend as well? This quiz was stupid and beginning to get on my nerves.

8. Has he told you he loves you?
a) Yes
b) No
c) He's just someone you go out with for a giggle
d) You don't love him

This was just so cringeworthy. . . .

9. Would you rather have a date with your mate than a date with your boy?
a) Yes
b) No
c) Depends on where you are going
d) You'd be happy to go out with them both at the same time

"I hope you're not expecting me to go into too much detail," I said.

"Listen—I do not want to know about you and

my brother's snogging sessions," Anna exclaimed, sticking her fingers in her ears. "La, la, la, la . . ."

"Like you think I'm going to tell you," I laughed.

10. **Could you live without a boy?**
a) No—never
b) Yes—but only while you suss out the talent
c) You always two-time anyway
d) Boys are only okay if you haven't got a good friend to chat with on the Net

That was it. Questions over. Brilliant! For some reason, these questions seemed a whole load more serious than the usual quizzes that Anna and I usually mucked about with.

"So, Beth," Anna said, her pen at the ready. "Got your pen poised? When you are ready . . . Question one: How often does he text you? . . ."

Chapter Two

How Often Do You See Him?

"*Beth? Earth calling* Beth?" Anna rolled her eyes upward. "Hello?"

Of course, I could hear her quite clearly. The problem was, I just wasn't sure I wanted to answer her.

"Sorry?" I said, pretending I really had been miles away in thought.

"*Der*, the quiz?"

"Oh, yes, sure," I mumbled.

"So. Question one again: How often does he text you?"

"Erm," I fudged, rolling my eyes up to the ceiling and counting vaguely with my fingers. What was the right answer to this question? Should I say that he sent me texts all the time, or would that look like we were one of those insufferable couples who couldn't be apart from each other? On the other hand, would saying that we only exchanged texts once a day sound as if we weren't really going out with each other? Yeah, but no, but . . . I dropped my hands into my lap.

"Beth?" Anna was getting irritated. "Do you want to do this or not?"

"Well—I don't mind, really."

"Oh, well, if that's how you feel, let's not bother." Anna chucked the magazine on her bed.

"Sorry," I sighed. "You know—with Joey . . . and you . . ."

"Are you okay?" Anna asked, arching her eyebrow up. Her perfectly plucked and shaped eyebrow that we had perfected for her just before Anna's sixteenth birthday.

"Course I am," I lied.

"Then why have you gone all strange?" Anna asked. She doesn't beat around the bush, this girl.

"I'm not being strange."

"Oh yeah?"

"Course not. Come on, let's do your nails," I suggested, wanting to change the subject and chill out again.

If I say so myself, I am very good at nails. Loads better, in fact, than Anna is. And Anna just *loves* being pampered and preened—but who doesn't? Anyway, it wasn't difficult to get Anna switched on to something else other than the quiz. What a relief.

I stayed at Anna's all afternoon and her nails looked gorgeous. I'd done them in an orangey-pink with sunray stripes sweeping across them. We'd found this brilliant kit in Gammons, our local department store. It had all these nail decorations in it that you just kind of pressed into the nail once it was painted—they looked really cool.

Anna was going to have a go at mine when hers were done, but then she decided she didn't want her own nails being smudged if she was fiddling with mine.

So I ended up doing my own because I could see her point—and anyway, I didn't want my handiwork to be spoiled.

After that, we stuffed our faces with some cookies that Anna found in one of her mum's kitchen cupboards, and then I realized that I should really get home to finish off some homework that I had abandoned earlier in the vain hope that ignoring it would make it go away.

I loitered as long as I could in the hallway of

Anna's house, hoping that Joey might appear any second. But he didn't.

So I cycled back to mine. But I couldn't resist stopping off at the twenty-four/seven shop on the corner before I went home to pick up my own copy of *Get It!* The quiz may have been over as far as Anna was concerned, but for me, it had only just begun.

Up in my room, I finished my homework. Okay, so I admit it, I'm one of those deadly boring kids who hates going to school without having all their work sorted. But I want to pass my exams. Partly because I just couldn't face my mum and dad groaning on and on if I fail them, but also I'd be really annoyed with myself as well. Anyway, I am not, sadly, one of those people who can breeze through exams without putting in the effort.

When I'd finished, and with all my school stuff shoved away back into my bag, I grabbed *Get It!* and headed straight for the page that had the quiz on it. I read the questions all over again. But I didn't bother to answer any of them. Instead, I went to the answers section—to the place where I reckoned I'd be looking at if I had bothered to answer the questions *honestly.*

Mostly Ds:
Well hey! You and your boy don't see much of each other, do you? Or maybe you are so laid back you like to make sure he knows you've got a life without him. But be warned: Don't be so chilled that he thinks you aren't interested!

What did that mean? I thought you shouldn't look too keen to see your boyfriend—you know, like a little puppy or someone who is completely desperate. But did Joey think that I didn't want to be with him? Maybe he did. Maybe that was why he hadn't been in touch with me today! Maybe it was my fault.

Suddenly my phone pinged, making me jump. It was a text—from Joey! Yah boo sucks to the quiz then!

SrE I MSd u. C u l8r in WEk XX

So I hadn't put him off! I texted him back:

OK! XX

He'd never sent me *two* kisses before. I couldn't resist sending him two kisses back!

"So we're going to Malaga for half-term with Guido." Frankie's voice floated across the canteen.

"Please, someone tell me I've become a character in a terrible made-for-DVD movie!" Anna groaned and slumped dramatically across the table, like a Victorian heroine in a really bad movie.

It was lunchtime, and because we'd had to go to the school office to see the bossy Mrs. Wilson to fess up to the fact that Anna had lost her lunch pass, we'd arrived in the hall later than everyone else. Of course, all the decent tables had gone, so the only table left was next to Frankie and the Franki-ettes. The Table of Doom that the entire school had successfully avoided and left—for us.

Anna made a moaning noise as the Franki-ettes made one of their gasps of admiring approval of Frankie's latest news installment. I put my hand over my mouth to cover up my own sniggering. Really, Frankie was too much—too, too much.

"What's the shoot for, Frankie?" Vic, another one of her groupies asked.

"To kill her—*bang*!" Anna hissed at me under her breath. I suppressed a giggle.

"I'm doing beachwear and sandals with Angelica," Frankie crooned. "You know—she's the girl in the Bright Eyes makeup campaign? Well, Guido insisted on working with us both. He said if we didn't do the shoot, then he just so wouldn't do it either."

"As if," Anna snorted into the table.

Frankie turned round and glared at me. She obviously thought it was me who had said it! I gave Anna a swift kick with my foot and a sweet, sweet smile to Frankie at the same time.

"Ouch!" Anna sat up. "What was that for?"

"Just eat your lunch and stop getting me into trouble." I giggled, and stuffed a mouthful of salad into my mouth.

Fortunately, La Frankie and Les Ettes were well ahead of us in the lunch-eating department, so they soon exited the school hall and left Anna and me in peace. But they made sure they gave us one of their "Never mind, some of you are destined to be saddos in life" looks as they went.

"She'd better watch out," Anna warned, eyeballing the Franki-ettes as they made their way outside. "If Frankie's not careful, she'll bash her big head on the double-door frame as she goes out."

I giggled. "Well, she's safe this time but maybe

she'll be in trouble by the time she gets back from Malaga and Guido and Angelica."

"She is insufferable!" Anna protested.

"Still, at least we'll have a giggle at her when she looks ridiculous in the new catalog. Some of those poses she strikes . . ." I said, sounding and feeling completely unconvinced. We all knew that, irritating as it was, Frankie was a looker.

We munched in silence at our chocolate gungy pudding (every Wednesday, and the only decent pudding of the week—a megamouthful of calories, but who cares?) for a few minutes before I said, "So, how's Sam?"

The pair had seemed pretty pleased with themselves when I'd last seen them at the end of one of the recent matches. Anna and I had gone to support Joey and Sam.

"He's okay," Anna confirmed. "Actually, he's more than okay, he's cool. And he's not a bad kisser, either."

Anna puckered her lips as if to offer a visual example of Sam's skills.

"Anna!" I squealed in embarrassment, turning around to check that no one was looking. Unfortunately, watching us were the odious duo of Baz and Greg (who, for some strange reason that neither

Anna nor I could remember, we had once thought were gorgeous but now realized were just geeks like most of the other boys in our school) and, on seeing Anna apparently blowing a kiss in their direction, blew one back at us.

"Gross!" I whined. "Now look what you've done—they probably still think we fancy them!"

"Oh, let them," Anna dismissed, picking up her tray. "It'll make their day. After all, no one else is going to fancy them. Come on, let's catch some of that sun before biology."

We stacked our trays on the rack and went outside to find a spot on one of the walls, where Anna immediately tilted her head up toward the sun.

"You shouldn't really be doing that," I said. "The sun will make your skin all wrinkly and age it prematurely."

"Yeah, yeah, and by the time I'm thirty I'll look like a three-hundred-year-old raisin," Anna said, stopping me before I could quote extracts from something I'd just read about skin cancer. "Don't worry, I put my new sunblock moisturizer on this morning. It's got an SPF of forty—so there! I've read the article in *Get It!* too, you know." She poked her tongue out at me and we both laughed.

I wanted to know more about Sam, though.

"So—do you see much of Sam, then?" I asked, trying to sound casual and as if I didn't really want or need to know the answer.

"A bit," Anna replied.

"Do you see him much in the week?"

"Hardly," Anna said. "I mean, by the time I've seen you and watched the telly—oh, and done my coursework—that doesn't leave huge amounts of time to see him, does it?"

"Oh—well, no."

I was a bit surprised that Anna counted seeing me as important—maybe *more* important—as seeing her boyfriend. Of course I was also pleased that she did.

"So, does Sam ring you much—to chat? You know, make arrangements for the weekend?"

"Sometimes, yeah." Anna turned her head from the sun and toward me, opening one eye. "What is this? Some kind of interrogation? Do you think I'm two-timing him with the god Greg?"

I blushed. "God—no way!"

"Maybe you think I'm three-timing him with Greg *and* Baz?" Anna giggled.

"Not unless you're desperate, no!" I laughed. "I don't know," I tried to explain. "I suppose I just wondered if you were happy to see Sam just on the weekends."

"I dunno," Anna said, standing up as the bell went, telling us all that the freedom of lunchtime was now over. "I suppose if I had more time and less stuff to do for school, maybe it would be nice to see more of him. But hey, Sam's got his stuff and his mates to sort too. So the weekends are just fine."

"Of course," I agreed.

"So," Anna suggested, taking her opportunity to quiz me. "How are things with my darling disgusting and gross brother?"

"Joey?" I asked, as if Anna had a choice of brothers that I was going out with. "Oh—fine. And he is most definitely *not* gross and disgusting. Yeah—fine. Anyway . . ." I paused. "You *know* . . ."

"I know what?" Anna demanded to know.

"Well . . ." I paused again to think. "Well—it's a bit difficult telling someone's sister why you fancy their brother or what he's like at kissing."

"Grief!" Anna pulled away from me dramatically as if I had some kind of lurgy. "Be quiet! I do not want to know details about my big brother's snogging skills!"

There were some boys from Year Eight sitting on the grass behind us. They guffawed when they heard Anna's outburst. Great! Now I really did blush.

"Anna!" I protested. "Give me a break!"

⊙

Much later that night, I lay in my bed, curtains drawn back, gazing out of the window and up at the stars. Was Joey, I wondered, looking at the same stars as me? Maybe Joey was reading a book? Or maybe he was talking to Sam about their respective girl-friends? A million thoughts about Joey seemed to run through my mind these days. I'd been going out with him for a few months now and I thought about him a lot. A lot more than I saw him, in fact.

But what puzzled me was that most of my thoughts were questions. Questions about what he thought about me and questions about what I ought to do when I was with him. As well as questions about what he was up to when he wasn't with me. Which was most of the time.

And my biggest question of all was why I didn't know the answer to any of them. I mean, how could I have a boyfriend for three months and still feel like I didn't know much about him? Was that normal? Was that how Anna was with Sam?

Chapter Three

Does He Have a Nickname for You?

Of course, Frankie gibbered on to anyone who would listen about her photo shoot.

Unfortunately, most people were dead impressed and said "Gosh! Wow! Tell me more!"—or that sort of thing—and Frankie, sadly, obliged.

She got a shock, though, when she was blabbing on about it just before our English lesson. For a teacher, Mrs. Stokes is quite cool. She kind of sees things differently from most other teachers. So when Mrs. Stokes came in and saw Frankie holding court with her worshippers, saying how she couldn't wait to be modeling full-time, Mrs. Stokes gave a kind of half smile.

"So sorry to interrupt you, Frankie, especially

when what you're saying is so important. But we have an English lesson to begin."

Even Frankie looked a tiny bit embarrassed. Well, only a tiny bit. But it only lasted a few minutes because, just when we were getting into some rhyming Shakespearian couplets, she started up again.

Mrs. Stokes said, "Do please excuse the rest of us interfering with your international modeling career, Frankie, but even supermodels need qualifications to fall back on, you know!" So Frankie shut up. Her cheeks even went a bit pink.

In a weird way, though, listening to Frankie drone on and on did break up the school day a bit. It was unbelievably irritating, of course—and I kind of hate admitting it—but it did make us stop thinking about exams and other boring stuff all the time.

"Listen," Anna said at break a couple of days later. "Nicky was telling me the other day about a special night they are doing in the salon next week. They're thinking of entering the place into some flashy high-profile competition. Everyone's buzzing about it."

Nicky was the really fit manager at the Cutting Room, who had given Anna her job there.

"Cool," I said. "Sounds fab."

"And, dear friend, we need hair to experiment on." Anna smiled sweetly at me and linked her arm through mine.

"Oh, no!" I said, trying to extract my arm from hers. Anna may have looked innocent but her grip was firm. Good job she was a mate—I reckoned those biceps could take on a sumo.

"What do you mean, 'no'?"

"Er—excuse me? Don't tell me you don't remember the last time you experimented on my hair!" I exclaimed. Did I really need to remind Anna about the time she attempted to put hair extensions on my hair, with such a disastrous effect that I had to have them cut out? As in, "Snip, snip—oops, you've got none of that hair left you had been growing out for ages." I'd ended up looking like a bog brush that had met the Toilet of Doom.

"But, Beth! That was totally different from this!" Anna protested.

"You must be joking if you think I'm going to be mad enough to let you loose on my hair again. NO!" And I meant it. I was beginning to get quite pleased with the way my hair was now. After months of growing it and nurturing it with conditioners and treatments (and a haircut from Nicky), it was beginning to look longer and thicker and—well, almost—glossy.

"But it wouldn't be me that played with it!" Anna urged. "Listen—I'm only one of the Saturday girls at the salon. Okay, I'm without a doubt the best Saturday girl they've got, but I won't be doing any hairstyles for the competition."

"So . . . what's the deal, then?" I asked suspiciously.

"Well," Anna said, back to smiling sweetly at me, "Nicky has asked if I could help him and the other stylists at the competition. How cool is that? We'll be going to London for it and everything."

"I still don't see what it's got to do with me," I said.

"Nicky wondered if you'd like to come along to the practice night at the salon," Anna explained. "He'll do your hair for you—free! Come on, Anna! Say you'll do it! It'll be fun and you'll look über-gorgeous, too!"

It was tempting, I had to admit. "But it's taken me ages to get my hair this long!" I stated. "I don't want it all chopped off!"

"No worries," Anna soothed. "Nicky doesn't want to do short, spiky looks. He says he wants to do longer hair. Like yours. So—you'll do it, then?"

Anna gave me one of her smiles. One that reminded me why she was my best friend who always made me laugh, always managed to make things seem better. But before I had a chance to reply, she said, "Excellent! We'll pop into the salon and let him know on our way home this afternoon. Anyway, I've kind of already said that you'll be doing it. . . ."

Somehow, I let Anna persuade me to go back to hers after school that day as well. After going to see Nicky, we were busy munching on some bread and jam in Anna's kitchen when the front door thudded shut and Joey appeared.

"Well, hello!" he said, bursting into the room. "Perfect timing, I see."

He grabbed my bread and stuffed it into his mouth. But I didn't care, because he gave me a beaming smile (I reckon it runs in the family) that clearly said: "It's great to see you but I can't really say that in front of my sister, can I?"

My heart gave a little flip and my brain gave a quick check on if my hair looked okay.

"Hi!" I said, turning round and buttering myself some more bread, then putting it down. I didn't want to look like I was a greedy pig, did I?

"So, what are you two up to?" Joey asked, oblivious to my abandoned sandwich.

I was about to tell him about the day at school but it really wasn't going to make a "hey, wow" conversation, was it? Why did I always have to think harder about what I was going to talk to Joey about than I did to Anna? Fortunately, Anna's snappy response saved me.

"Oh, checking out our new Rolex watches, listening to the iPods we were given to try out for *Get It!*, and talking about the nightclub we went to last night. You?"

"Another usual day at school then, eh?" Joey laughed and grabbed the knife from me to make himself some more to snack on. He winked at me as he did, and my heart did a little jump. God, he was so gorgeous that it would be impossible to remember quite how gorgeous he was unless I could stare at him all day.

"What about you?" I asked. "Had a good day at college?"

Joey went to the sixth form college in town. He did go to our school before, but had left after GCSEs.

"Not bad, not bad," Joey explained, and flipped the kettle on. "Usual tutor groups and stuff. Nothing too exciting. But we did have a pea fight in the canteen that I won hands-down. Excellent."

"A pea fight?" I asked.

"Yeah—it was so funny. You know, with Sam's peas. Flick, flick?" Joey gestured with his hands to explain. "It did get a bit out of control though, with everyone else joining in."

"You are joking?" Anna said, sounding as if she already knew that he wasn't.

"Didn't you get into trouble?" I asked.

"Trouble?" Joey questioned, raising one eyebrow in a particularly cute way.

"All those peas being flicked around the canteen? Mrs. Firesmith would go bonkers if we did that," I said, realizing as I said it that someone as charming as Joey was unlikely to get in trouble.

Mrs. Firesmith is the head dinner lady at school and she is quite terrifying. It's "ladles at dawn" with Mrs. Firesmith if anyone smashes a plate—even if it is a genuine accident.

"Don't remind me about Mrs. Firesmith!" Joey said, shying backward and making a cross with his fingers as if he was reeling back from a vampire. "The only dinner lady that can turn a baked bean into a bullet!"

We all giggled. "So you didn't get told off?"

"Nah!" Joey said, wiping his jammy hands on the tea towel. "It was just a laugh—and I promise, cross my heart, that I helped to tidy up afterward."

"Oh, sure you did," Anna said sarcastically. "Come on, Beth—shall we chill out upstairs?"

"Erm . . ." That one stumped me. I was kind of hoping that now that I had the chance of seeing Joey, I could spend a bit more time with him. Only I didn't want to make a fool of myself—it was too embarrassing in front of Anna for a start. And, anyway, what if Joey had something else to do and didn't want to see me?

"Sorry," Joey said. "You can't."

"What do you mean, we can't?" Anna frowned hard at her brother.

"You can't go upstairs, not yet," Joey moved toward me and put his arm around me. I melted into his shoulder. "Well, *you* can go upstairs and chill out on your own, Anna. In fact, that's a great plan. Go on, run along. Beth and I are going to catch up on stuff down here."

I felt his warmth as his arm enveloped me—and I wasn't complaining.

"Sorry, I'm sure," Anna said, pretending to be offended but flashing me a grin. "Don't mind me." She walked out of the kitchen, waving her hand backward at me. "See you upstairs when you're allowed out, Beth."

I giggled and looked up at Joey's face. He smiled down at me.

"So, you," he said, pulling me into his chest with a bear hug.

"So, you, too," I said, still looking up at him, trying to stop myself from smiling too much.

"It's good to see you," Joey said. "I missed you on Sunday."

I was slightly surprised, because he said it as if *I* was the one that hadn't turned up to see *him*. But I didn't want to say anything and sound like I was nagging. "Yes, me too," I said.

"Come on," Joey flicked the kettle back on, behind me. "Let me make you a drink and then we can play my new Xbox game."

"Cool."

We did that for an hour or so. It was a game that I hadn't played before, but I was actually quite good at it and we'd been having a good laugh playing it. Then Anna came down in a huff.

"I thought we were going to do that French homework together," she said rather grumpily.

"Oops, sorry," I said, extracting myself from my proximity to Joey on the sofa, and looking at my watch. Sometimes this situation was really tricky. I felt bad for having blown Anna out, and it must be weird for her seeing her best mate and her brother all snuggled up on the sofa.

"Teacher's pets," Joey joked. "Go on, Beth—better

help Anna or she'll never be able to understand it."

"Hey, you!" Anna said, cuffing her brother across the head.

"Sorry, Anna, I didn't realize we'd been that long," I explained. "See you later?" I asked Joey.

"Sure, Beth," Joey replied, giving me one of his delicious smiles.

The French turned out to be easier than we'd thought and we polished it off quite quickly, thank goodness. I shoved my books back into my rucksack and looked at my watch again, groaning when I realized what the time was.

"I'd better go or my mum will kill me. I should have been back about half an hour ago to look after Jack."

"Glad you could fit me in," Anna commented, her voice uncharacteristically sharp.

"Sorry?"

"Well—if it's not Joey then it's Jack you want to be with instead of me."

"Anna, I *have* to be back with Jack—believe me, if I had a choice I'd much rather be with you than my baby brother. You know that," I spluttered.

"Don't you mean you'd rather be with my big brother?" Anna said with a glint in her eye.

I looked at her but didn't know what to say. It was

a difficult question because I actually wanted to be with them both. Not at the same time, of course. But I liked being with both of them.

"Anna—it's not like that," I tried to explain. "It's just I don't see much of Joey. I don't get the chance, do I? Just like you and Sam." I looked anxiously at my watch. My mum really *was* going to kill me.

"Oh, forget it, Beth. Sorry, I'm just in a grump." Anna smiled. "You'd better get back to Jack. Let's hope he hasn't done anything 'home alone' to get you into trouble!"

"Don't even think it!" I laughed, tumbling down the stairs with Anna behind me.

"You off, then?" Joey came out of the living room, where he was obviously still playing on the Xbox.

"Yeah," I said, slipping my coat off the banister and onto my shoulders. "See you, then."

I looked at Anna and then at Joey. I was kind of hoping to say good-bye to Joey on my own, but after what she'd just said I didn't want to look like I was giving Anna the cold shoulder.

"Haven't you got someone to send a text to?" Joey asked Anna, as if he had read my mind.

"Oh—so sorry to keep being in the way in my own home!" Anna sighed. "See you, Beth!" She ran back upstairs to her room.

Joey looked at me and smiled.

"Great to see you," he said, putting his arms round my waist.

"Yes," I agreed. "See you soon?"

"Hope so," Joey said.

"See you, then," I said, pulling myself away from him.

"Bye." He leaned down to me and gave me a soft kiss. Not one of those sloppy, sticky ones. More of a gently lingering one. It was nice.

I opened the door and slipped onto the doorstep.

"Bye, Jo-Jo," I said, turning to look behind me.

"Jo-Jo?" Joey replied. "Who's Jo-Jo?"

"Sorry?"

He sounded irritated with me. I blushed.

"You called me Jo-Jo," Joey pointed out, like I really needed to be reminded. "It makes me sound like something from *CBeebies* or *Ballamory*!"

"Yes, no . . . sorry . . ."

"See you."

"Bye, Joey," I said. But it was too late. He'd already gone inside and shut the door.

When I got home, I stomped up to my room, feeling cross and sorry for myself at the same time. I grabbed the copy of *Get It!* and turned straight to the quiz again, question three.

3. Does he have a nickname for you?
a) Yes
b) Only in private
c) When he's feeling romantic
d) No

I guessed that as Joey didn't like me calling him Jo-Jo, there was no way he was going to have a nickname for me, was there?

Chapter Four

What's Your Idea of
a Perfect Date?

"Guess what?" Anna said urgently, a couple of days later on the bus in to school. Luckily, we'd gotten over the incident the other day about Joey.

"Umm," I replied thoughtfully. "You've been picked as the reserve for the England team in the first round of the World Cup?"

"In my dreams!" Anna sighed, closing her eyes at the thought of getting that close to David Beckham. "No—guess again!"

I looked at her sideways and raised my eyebrow in thought. "Can I ask the audience?"

"Oh, for goodness' sake—give up! You'll never guess, anyway," Anna said dramatically. "Listen!" She leaned closer toward me as if she was about to tell me some enormous secret. "Sam called me last night!"

There was a theatrical pause as she looked at me, her eyes wide.

"Well that's nice," I said. "Er—I imagine this isn't the first time he's rung you?"

"As if, Beth!" Anna retorted. "No, listen—you remember we saw that gig advertised? The seventies tribute night? Well, when I saw Sam at the weekend, I told him how I'd really love to go to it. You'll never guess!"

"I think we've already established that I never will," I laughed.

"Well, Sam rang me last night to tell me that he's bought tickets for us to go! How fab is that?"

"Wow, that's great, Anna," I agreed. And it was—the poster for the gig promised a really good night. "So when are you going?"

"It's on the Friday in a couple of weeks' time," Anna explained. "Mum's quite cool about it. She says it's up to me because I'm the one who has got to get up early on Saturday morning to go to work."

"Well, that's true," I commiserated, knowing how Anna struggled as much as I did with having to get up early on Saturday as well as every other day of the week. "But hey, it's going to be worth it."

"Mum says she's got some old clothes from the seventies that she's going to lend me. But you've got to promise me you'll help me with my makeup on the night?"

"Sure," I giggled. "And we could frizz up your hair with those old hair crimpers of my mum's!"

"Thanks!" Anna said, rummaging in her bag. "Oh no!"

"What's up now?" I asked.

"My geography sheet! I've left it at home—and I was going to do my homework now!"

"Oh, Anna!" I groaned and picked up my own bag and started to delve. "Here—use mine."

"Thanks, Beth." She smiled at me. "You're a mate!"

Much later on that night, I was sitting in my room, pratting around with a computer game and doing really badly because I wasn't really concentrating on it.

Instead, I was thinking. About the things that had happened, and not happened, in the last week or so. I'd done most of my work but I hadn't heard from Joey, not since I'd seen him when I'd been round at Anna's the other afternoon. I hadn't got in touch with him—but things had been so hectic with Anna, and homework, and my Saturday job.

Why did I have to be such a pencil case rather

than one of those girls at school who always seemed to be out having a good time and hardly bothered about being late with their coursework? I'd be much happier to be like Anna. I mean, she knows how to balance having a good time *and* how to get on with her school stuff. And from what she said about Sam, she also knows how to keep a boyfriend interested in her when he isn't actually standing in front of her.

I have to say, I was dead-impressed with the way Anna had not only told Sam that she'd have liked to go to the concert but that he had gone out and gotten the tickets to take her. How cool was that?

I couldn't remember once telling Joey what I was interested in since I'd been going out with him. We tended to talk about what was on telly or his football or computer games.

I tried to remember whether I'd ever told him the kind of stuff I was into *before* I went out with him, but I don't think I could have, on account of the fact that I never really had *conversation* conversations with him before we went out.

Why was it so weird, though? Before we'd been going out together I'd been able to talk to Joey about anything and everything. Since then, I worried so much about what I said to him now that he was my boyfriend. Seeing as I wanted to be with Joey so much, why did being with him make me so self-conscious? So *bothered*. It was so much easier just being with Anna.

Everything seemed very messy in my head.

I was still clicking idly on my mouse when I got zapped by a purple-and-yellow striped caterpillar with sticky-out spikes. The screen in front of me dissolved into a melting molten mass and some doom-laden music oozed out.

I shut the game down and grabbed my copy of *Get It!* I had looked at the "Suit Him or Boot Him?" quiz so often now that the pages just fell open in the right place.

Okay, so I'd already established that Joey was most definitely not into nicknames. If he reacted so strongly to me giving him one, it was a good guess that he wasn't likely to start calling me Tigger or something. Okay, I know that being called Tigger would be pretty awful. I mean, it would sound like you spent your life bouncing around in an irritating way, wouldn't it? Suddenly I felt loads better about the nickname thing. It had sounded quite cute—all right, romantic—when I'd first thought about it when I read the quiz. Now it just seemed a bit daft. Positively stupid, in fact. Clearly, it was loads better not to have a nickname myself, and not to have a nickname for Joey. Joey and Beth sounded just fine. Joey and Beth. Beth and Joey. There. That was that question sorted.

I glanced down at the next question.

4. What's your idea of a perfect date?

To be honest, I'm not sure that I'd ever really thought about what my ideal date was until I'd read the question in the magazine. Never having had a boyfriend before, it hadn't really occurred to me that a date could be anything other than perfect. I'd just kind of assumed that all dates were loads of fun. Unless of course you were going out with:

a) a boy from Year Eight—any boy from Year Eight

b) someone who took themselves so seriously they never laughed at themselves (or other people, come to think of it)

c) the kind of person who thought it was hysterically funny to wear false teeth in class at every registration or something equally weird

d) someone like my disgusting younger brother (who would clearly never get a

girlfriend on account of the fact that he
was such an idiot).

I thought back to the dates that I'd had with Joey. Rather depressingly, I realized that there weren't that many where we had actually gone out.

Anna and I had gone to see Sam and Joey play football a few times and had gone for a burger afterward. Joey had also taken me with him to choose his new football boots. Other than that, we kind of spent our time together just hanging out, either in the park or round at Anna's.

Joey had come back to my house once and it had been hellish. Not because of Joey, though. No, it was my mum and my kid brother, Jack, who had made it so excruciatingly embarrassing.

First my mother. When Joey and I had gone back to my house after a football match, Mum had tried to make out she was incredibly laid back about Joey being there. But she so wasn't. Mum's known Joey as long as she's known Anna, but she suddenly became all chummy and told Joey how welcome he was and how he could pop round any time, even if I wasn't here. What was all that about? I don't know who was more embarrassed—me or Joey.

Then Mum came out with a cringeworthy "our

home is your home" speech and then seemed to be completely freaked out when Joey took her literally and wore his trainers into the living room. Now, if I make it clear that Mum and Dad got a new carpet a year ago, that the carpet is cream-colored, that even my dad isn't allowed into the room without shoes and only if he is wearing certain socks (yes, after a whole year!), imagine how uncool my mum was about Joey in his trainers. Please!

Then my mum appeared with a plate of muffins that, for one desperate moment, I thought she was going to pretend she had made herself. Chocolate muffins. Great to eat. And good for crumbs. On cream carpet. Mum, who made about three million excuses for needing to "just pop in" to the living room while we watched *The Weakest Link*, with her hand-held rechargeable vacuum. And all the time she was trying to make out that it "didn't matter in the slightest."

Then there was the problem with my desperate brother who, for some reason, seemed to think that it was really funny that I had a boyfriend. You see, Jack seemed to believe that absolutely no one would want to go out with me.

So he kept running into the room (correction: at

first, he just wouldn't *leave* the room and in the end had to be bribed by my mum with a double chocolate chip cookie plus a Chocolate Feast ice cream) and asking, "Are you really Beth's boyfriend?" When Joey said yes, Jack asked, bewildered, "Why?" Joey seemed to think it was funny.

Unfortunately, I didn't. Normally, I would have thumped Jack and then completely denied it when the little snitch blabbed to Mum. This time, I couldn't because it wouldn't have looked very cool to bash my annoying little brother in front of Joey, would it?

The course of true love didn't seem to be that easy to organize. I looked back at the quiz. Question four was throbbing on the page at me, begging for an answer.

4. What's your idea of a perfect date?

Well, what *was* my idea of a perfect date? Hmm . . . I guessed they meant what was my idea of a perfect date if Joey and I had all the money in the world to spend on it. In that case, maybe a trip on Eurostar to Paris for a quick whiz up the Eiffel Tower and then a spot of lunch. During this perfect date, I would, natch, be fluent in French. Oh, and wearing the latest designer jeans and a pair of Jimmy Choos.

Alternatively, a visit to the London Eye could be quite cool, followed by a no-expense-spared shopping trip to Harvey Nichols—a shop that I'm always reading about in my mum's magazines as *the* place to buy designer stuff.

Mmm, nice.

Or maybe a trip to the theater to see a musical, popping in, of course, to see the stars in their dressing rooms afterward before we went off for a stuff-your-face meal at Jamie Oliver's. Lovely.

Sadly, I had to admit that I did not have the dosh for a money-no-object date. Nor did Joey. But I did have enough to go to the cinema. And the latest Jude Law film was released this Thursday. The guy who does the movie show on the telly said it was brilliant and Jude Law is gorgeous. So that would make a pretty good date with Joey this Friday. So I decided it was time to be proactive about all this for once. I reached for my phone to give him a call.

"Hi, Beth. How're you doing?"

"Fine. Great," I replied. "You?"

"Just cruising," he confirmed, sounding totally unstressed. "So what can I do you for?"

"Well, I was just wondering if you were free on Friday evening. That new Jude Law film is out then

and I thought we could go. It's meant to be really brilliant." I left barely a gigasecond before I carried on. "So
what do you think? Shall we go? I could get the times
off the Internet."

"Jude Law? No thanks, Beth. I don't think so.
Nah."

"Oh well," I said, trying not to sound disap-
pointed. "I just thought you might be free on
Friday, that's all."

"Not for a Jude Law film, Beth, no, sorry," Joey
replied. "I don't think it's worth missing football
training for a girly film. If you were thinking about
Killer Demon 9, then maybe," he laughed.

"Ha, ha," I joined in. I didn't want him to think I
was getting moody about it. "Sure."

"Listen—gotta go," Joey said, still cheerful. "Dad's
calling me for supper and I'm a growing boy. See ya!"

"Sure," I replied, trying to sound like I was smiling
with pleasure that Joey had called a Jude Law film
"girly."

"Oh," Joey added before he pressed end. "And
thanks for calling."

"Yeah, bye," I said lamely.

I sat down on my bed, my phone still limp in my
hand. How would *Get It!* rate the call, I wonder?
Certainly not a ten out of ten for megabrilliantness.

Nor a nine, I reckoned, because Joey hadn't said he'd go out with me. Or eight, or seven. Or even six. I might just get five out of ten for calling him. On the other hand, I had to remind myself, he had accused me of trying to choose a "girly" film. And I imagine that would only get me a four out of ten if I was lucky. Which I certainly didn't feel. . . .

Chapter Five

What's His Idea
of a Perfect Date?

In the end, I went to see the film with Anna.

"Ooooo, Jude Law is just so cute," I said when we jumped onto the bus home.

"He is simply divine," Anna agreed. "Quite frankly, his talent is lost on anyone else but me. Wasted."

"Someone," I giggled, "as modest and understated as you, that's for sure."

"So what did you think?" Anna asked me. "Stand up, sit down, or pass out?"

Anna and I always like to rate films like they do in *Hello!* You know, when they have the picture of the woman who loves the film so much she stands up to applaud? And she sits down to clap if it's just good but faints if it's terrible?

I thought for a bit and then said, "I reckon it's somewhere between standing up and sitting down. Kind of knees bent but not quite standing up—don't you?"

"Yeah, probably," Anna agreed. "I mean, Jude Law is so cute you'd give him a standing-up any day, but the plot was a bit dodgy a couple of times."

"A bit obvious, true," I confirmed. "But I really enjoyed it—I wouldn't have wanted to miss it."

"Nah."

We were distracted for a few seconds by some woman who was making a huge fuss about a speck of dirt on her bus seat. She looked like a Barbie doll because she was so made up—even though she was pretty old. Way too old to be dressed like that. She looked, I guess, "girly."

"Anna?" I wondered.

"That's me. What?"

"Did you think that was a girly film?"

Anna turned and looked at me, a puzzled expression on her face. "You what?"

"I said, did you think that was girly film? You *know*," I emphasized.

The look on Anna's face didn't alter much when

she replied, "Well, not being a 'girly,'" she said sarcastically, "I'm not sure I'd agree that it was a 'girly' film." She looked pensive for a minute and then said, "No—I don't think it was a 'girly' flick. Definitely not. There was loads of action. What about that car chase? Nothing girly about that."

After Joey's condemnation of it, I felt relieved. "No, I don't think so either."

"But what made you ask if it was girly?" Anna asked.

"Oh it was just something someone said," I mumbled dismissively, hoping to end the subject.

"What? About you being girly or the film?" Anna interrogated.

"Yes—no."

"Sorry? Yes? No? Is it you or the film that's girly?"

"Oh, honestly, Anna, let's forget it," I said, slightly irritated—although I don't know why, because Anna was only reacting the way I would have. "I suppose I just wondered if you thought it was the sort of film boys would like. As much as we did."

"Oh." Anna looked more thoughtful. "Dunno, really. I suppose boys are meant to be more into thrillers and spy movies than films about love. But I don't see why that should always be true. After all, we both like a good James Bond movie as much as anyone else, don't we?"

She was, of course, right.

"Do you think Sam would have enjoyed it?" I asked.

"James Bond, defo. Jude Law, though? Who knows?" Anna said. "Who cares? Would Sam have liked it? Probably not—I mean, Joey would have hated it. He can't even stand watching *Friends*."

"No," I said, pretending to giggle with acknowledged acceptance.

Joey couldn't stand *Friends*? I had no idea. I love *Friends* and I've watched all the repeats—and the repeats of the repeats—on Channel 4. It had never occurred to me that Joey wouldn't want to giggle through it with me. But then, I suppose I'd never even thought about it either. Was that good or bad? Was that something I should have known about my boyfriend, I wondered? Or was that something I shouldn't have thought about—like I hadn't?

"Beth? Hello? Beth? Earth calling Beth?"

"Sorry?" I turned round as Anna tapped me on my shoulder to see her standing up.

"This is our stop," Anna explained.

"Ooops!"

Seconds later, we hopped off and headed for home.

I'd kind of gotten used to having to wake up early on Saturday mornings so that I could go and work at Shopalot. Don't get me wrong—I would gladly have ignored the alarm, turned over, and gone on to have another couple of hours' sleep. But, actually, I quite enjoyed work. It was quite nice to be somewhere that you weren't treated like a kid. And, more important, I liked the cash that you got at the end of the day. The manager had this little system where you went along to his office during the afternoon tea break and collected your pay in cash. When I got that in my purse, the waking up bit was completely forgotten and replaced by the long list of things I wanted to be able to buy.

When I first worked in the supermarket, I was a shelf-stacker for the breakfast cereal aisles. Now, I had kind of been promoted to the chill counter and I filled up all the yogurts and stuff like that. I also got a chance to sit at the till at the end of the day, which was quite cool.

Some people were just so nice—others spoke to you like you were their personal slave. Whatever, the people were all different, and they bought loads of food, which meant I was always restocking, so the afternoon passed really quickly.

This particular afternoon, though, there was more action in the supermarket than usual. I told Anna all about it when I met up with her at the bus stop after work so that we could go home together.

"You will never guess what happened today!" I stated, dead dramatic.

"Well it can't have been Brad Pitt coming in, because he came to see us for some highlights." Anna grinned.

"Oh, ha, ha!"

"Go on—no idea," Anna conceded. "Tell me."

"This woman only went and tried to pinch a frozen turkey," I started to explain, but the thought of it was making me giggle.

"So she got caught, then?" Anna stated the obvious.

"Well—yes, but you will never guess how!" I added some drama to my story.

"Don't tell me she dropped it as she got to the door."

"Nope," I continued. "She'd stuffed the turkey up her front and pretended she was pregnant, but the security guard had seen her come in looking all slim and slinky and had spotted her heading to the exit looking eight months gone. The look on his face was brilliant!"

"No! Never!"

We both giggled helplessly as we carried on waiting for the bus to finally come.

"Can you imagine how cold it must have been?" I said, tears sliding down my cheeks.

We were laughing so much that I didn't realize my phone was ringing at first. I eventually answered it as Anna and I stepped onto the bus and flashed our passes at the driver.

It was Joey.

"Wotcha!" he said. "What you up to?"

"Hiya—just on my way home from work," I explained, still with a giggle in my voice. "What about you?"

"Listen, I'm just hanging out with Sam and we were thinking of going to the disco at the college tonight. D'you fancy coming?"

"Who's that?" Anna mouthed as we sat down at the back of the bus.

"It's Joey," I said. "He wants to know if we want to go with him and Sam to the college disco tonight."

"Mmm." Anna thought. "Yeah—maybe. You?"

As if I was going to turn Joey down!

"You still there, Beth?" Joey asked. "Not that I want to interrupt you two girls or anything."

"Sorry," I apologized. "Sure—the disco sounds okay."

"Great," Joey said. He sounded really pleased that

I'd said yes, and that made me feel good. "How about the three of us pick you up at about seven thirty, then?"

"Sure—see you then. Bye!"

I'd worry about sorting it out with my mum later. More important, what was I going to wear?

"Hello, Mrs. Clarkson. How are you?" Joey gave my mum a beaming smile and she was instantly putty in his hands.

"Very well indeed, Joey, thank you. Hello, Anna!" she said. "And you must be Sam."

"Hello," Sam said, and shook her hand. "Nice to meet you."

"Shall we go, then? Bye, Mum," I said, shuffling myself around my mum to get out of the hall.

"Oh." Mum seemed almost surprised. As if she was actually expecting us all to come in and sit down for a cup of tea on the sofa. *Oh no, no, no!* "Well, have a great time, then. See you back here at eleven, Beth. No later."

She made me sound like a baby and I could feel my face flush with embarrassment.

"Mrs. Clarkson?" Joey carried on smiling at Mum. "Do you think we could make it eleven thirty? I promise that we will bring Beth safely home. Please?"

"Well." Mum gave it some thought while Joey

practiced his most trustworthy expression on her. "Okay, then—but no later. And if there are any problems, please make sure you phone, Beth!"

"Sure," I said. I couldn't get out of the place quick enough. "See you, Mum!"

"So, how are you, then?" Joey said, putting his arm around me as we set off on our walk toward the college.

"Fine, thanks." I smiled back. And I certainly did feel fine walking along with Joey. "How about you?"

"You know." Joey grinned down at me. "I feel great. Good. Glad that I am walking along with you to this disco-thingy. You look great, by the way."

"Thanks," I said. It had only taken me forty-five minutes to decide what to wear and the entire contents of my wardrobe were now open-plan-filed across my bedroom floor. Why was I so bothered, when Joey had already seen me in my scruffiest gear?

But hearing Joey say I looked great made it all worth it. I actually felt terrific.

The college hall, where the disco was being held, was absolutely packed. There were loads of people there and a couple of times I got worried that I was going to end up getting split up from the others.

If I'd been hoping for a chance of getting Joey to myself, I was out of luck because it seemed that he and Sam knew virtually everyone at the disco and spent most of their time chatting to people as if they were all their best friends.

Anna and I tried to talk a couple of times but the music was so loud that we had to shout. The DJ was really cool, though, and he played some great tracks. So Anna and I danced away, with Sam and Joey sometimes joining us.

Of course, at the end, a couple of slow tracks were played and I panicked a little when I heard their familiar opening chords. I wasn't sure that Joey would be into slow dancing. And I certainly didn't want to find myself on the dance floor, embarrassingly on my own.

It turned out that I needn't have bothered because Joey was absolutely fine about it. But toward the middle of the second slow number, Joey broke away from me and looked at his watch.

"Come on, then," he said, beckoning over to Sam and Anna to come with us. "We'd better get going. We promised your mum we'd be back by eleven thirty."

"Thanks," I said, feeling instantly humiliated. *Thanks, Mum*, I thought.

Joey didn't seem to mind. But I felt like a total

kid who was being taken home to Mummy. None
of the others seemed to have a curfew to get home
by. At least, if they did, they weren't mentioning it.

Pretty soon, we all had our jackets back on and were
walking back to mine.

Joey and Sam seemed to still be full of life as they
bounced along the pavement ahead of Anna and me,
messing about and trying to put each other in various
dustbins along the way.

"What a pair of idiots," Anna said, linking her
arm through mine and shivering as we trotted on in
the cool night air.

You couldn't help laughing at them, though,
because they were funny. And clearly, they were enjoying themselves. Anna and I started to gossip about
some of the girls and the things that we'd seen going on
during the evening, which really had been fun, even if
I hadn't seen much of Joey.

It was good to catch up on all the chat that we
couldn't have during the disco on account of not being
able to hear. We were so into a serious goss session
about one particular girl that we were, to be honest,
being really nasty about her to-die-for hair and
sensational jeans, that we suddenly realized that Joey
and Sam were nowhere to be seen.

"Where are they?" I asked the air as Anna and I stopped dead in our tracks.

"Where've they gone?" Anna wondered.

We looked around us, turning to look behind us. Could Sam and Joey have got behind us? I didn't think so.

"What are they up to?" I said, pulling myself closer in to Anna in the chill.

Apart from the sound of the odd car, the street was silent.

"Oh, come on," Anna said. "We'll catch up with them somewhere."

"Yeah," I agreed, and we walked on ahead.

We walked in silence for a bit and then Anna said, "What was that?"

"What?"

"That kind of . . . scratching noise," Anna explained. "My mum'll go bonkers if she finds out Joey's gone off and left us."

I hope my mum never finds out, I thought. I'd be terminally grounded if she knew I was walking home on my own with Anna.

"There—that's the noise again," Anna hissed.

"I didn't hear it."

"You must have!" she spluttered. "It came from just ahead of us. I'm sure it did."

Then I did hear it. It was *definitely* a scratching noise. "Omigod, what was it?"

We both stopped dead in our tracks and listened. After a couple of seconds of silence there was a sort of shuffling noise—like something was moving in the bushes.

"It's probably a cat," I said, trying to sound far more confident than I felt. "Come on—let's find Sam and Joey."

We walked briskly on, only to hear a kind of hooting noise. Not like an owl, but a bit like a bird, anyway.

"What the heck was that?!" we both said at the same time.

"Where are those two?" I wanted to know, feeling kind of angry that they weren't there to help us.

The hooty noise came again and this time seemed much closer. Just as I was beginning to get suspicious about this bird-cat that we seemed to be hearing there was this kind of explosion of activity both in front of and behind us.

"Gotcha!" Sam screamed from in front of us whilst Joey did the same from behind.

"Aaaaah!" I screamed, my heart pounding in shock.

"Waaaah!" yelled Anna, spinning me round so that she could look behind us.

Sam and Joey were collapsing into helpless laughter. A window in a nearby house was yanked open above our heads.

"Clear off, you lot!" a man yelled. "Go on— before I call the police!"

I was mortified. If my mum knew what we were up to she would go ape.

"Come on!" I hissed and yanked Anna along.

The boys followed us, still laughing. Laughing so much that Anna joined in. As my heart slowed back to its more normal beat, I also began to see the funny side and started to giggle.

"You should have seen your faces!" Joey spluttered between laughter.

"Yeah," Sam agreed. "They were priceless! And it was so easy—you were yakking away so much you didn't even notice when we hid!"

"Oh, ha, ha!" Anna retorted. "I bet you'd have been just as scared if we'd done it to you!"

"Yes—I bet!" I said. "Scaredy-cats!"

"No way!" Joey replied. "We," he pulled Sam close toward him and they puffed out their shoulders and squared their chests in tandem, "are not scared of anything."

"Oh, I bet you are!" Anna laughed.

"We'll find something," I said, sounding far more confident than I realized I felt as soon as I'd said it. I mean, how were we going to scare them?

We were still giggling, though, as we got close to my house.

"Got it!" Anna said as we turned the corner of my street.

"Got what?" I asked.

"The London Dungeons!" Anna exclaimed. "They say that's really seriously scary. Why don't we go? It'd be cool."

"I'm not sure," I mumbled. I'd read that it really *was* scary. And full of rats. *Live* rats.

"I'm chilled," Sam said. "When are we going to go, then?"

"How about next weekend?" Joey said, looking quite cheery about it.

"Can't," I commented, feeling relieved. "We'll be at work." I nodded toward the boys. "Anyway, you will be too, won't you?"

Both Sam and Joey had jobs at a local garden center. That was sorted.

"We'll go on Sunday, then," Sam said.

And despite my best efforts, it was agreed.

Chapter Six

Is He a Grown-Up— or a Groan-Up?

"*Why on earth* did you have to suggest the London Dungeons?" I grumbled at Anna down the phone the next day.

I'd looked it up on the Internet that morning. Not only was it dead expensive, it sounded pretty horrible—and maybe scary, too.

"I mean," I moaned on, "it has live rats!"

"I know! It sounds fab, doesn't it?" Anna said.

"You *want* to see rats?"

Was it just me? Had the world gone mad?

"Oh, give over," Anna replied. "It's not as if the rats are going to be running free around our feet, is it?"

"I do hope not," I said, feeling sick at the thought.

"I mean—do you think they still carry the plague?" I was only half joking.

Anna giggled. "Don't be daft! It wouldn't be allowed, for a start," she said. "Well, at least—I don't think it would. Listen, it'll be a laugh."

"Course," I lied.

"We'll all have fun. I bet you," Anna said with certainty.

But I really didn't fancy a rat running over my foot. . . . Anyway, not wanting to think about things that had whiskers and maybe even fleas, I changed the subject.

"So, how are things with you and Sam?"

"Okay," Anna said.

"Just okay?" I wanted to know. Anna was always so matter-of-fact about Sam. She never seemed to be particularly excited about having a boyfriend. But then, she never seemed to find being with him awkward, either.

"Yeah—no—everything's fine, Beth," Anna concluded. "You know—he's a boy. Into bloke stuff loads of the time. He's also a laugh and good fun to be with. You know."

"Sure," I said.

"Why do you want to know?" Anna asked. "Everything's all right with my darling bro, isn't it?"

"Course," I said. "Joey's great. And very cute."

"Oh, please—there's no need to go that far."

I giggled. "But it's true. Joey's great. His shock of blond hair and that cute little grin that makes me feel weak at the knees when he flashes it at me."

"Enough!" Anna wailed, and I giggled some more before we said our farewells and put the phone down.

I lay down on my bed and sighed. Joey *was* great and everything I'd just said to Anna was true. But it was beginning to be a bit of a pain going out with my best friend's brother, because suddenly there were just heaps of things that I couldn't talk about with her. And talking about your boyfriend with your best friend is what having a best friend is all about, no?

"So," Anna squeezed in between mouthfuls of pasta at lunch a couple of days later, "Nicky called me last night and said he wondered if you could go along one evening this week to see him about this competition."

"Well, I don't know," I said. "I'll have to see if I have a window in my diary." I pretended to retrieve an invisible diary from my rucksack. "Is there any day in particular that is good for Nicky?"

Anna rolled her eyes at me. "He said Thursday would be good—so how about it?"

"Well, what do you know? Thursday appears to be the only opportunity I have!"

Anna giggled. "Thursday it is, then. Anyway, I couldn't do Friday because that's when I'm going to the seventies gig night with Sam."

"Anna!" The grating tones of Frankie's voice made us both sit up.

There stood Frankie, behind Anna, with all her Franki-ettes in attendance around her. I looked up at them all with their identical hair, and their identical way of flipping up the collar on their school shirts and doing up their ties. Ugggh!

Anna dug determinedly into her meal, not looking up.

"Anna?" Frankie was clearly puzzled that Anna hadn't immediately turned around to respond. I suppressed a little giggle.

"Anna?" she squeaked again.

Anna tossed her fork down on her plate and heaved herself around, looking like it was an enormous effort to do so.

"Yes? What do you want?"

Frankie's bottom lip wobbled for a nanosecond. She wasn't used to being greeted without her usual doting admiration. Actually, correct that: Frankie couldn't *understand* that everyone didn't want to adore her. But Frankie was a professional—you had to hand it to her. A grin fixed across her face as she looked down from her heavenly superior position and addressed Anna again.

"Hey, Anna—how are you?" Her sincere face now replaced the grin.

"Like you care," Anna said flippantly.

Like a squirrel at a nut, Frankie wasn't going to give up that easily.

"I just love your hair, Anna," Frankie intoned, leaning ever so close to Anna's face. "It just looks so luscious these days. Now that you work at the Cutting Room."

Anna looked at Frankie, her expression unchanging.

"Doesn't it?" Frankie turned to her tribe, who all nodded their heads enthusiastically and grinned in agreement.

"Sorry—do you think you could give me a bit more space?" Anna asked, leaning back. "What do you want, Frankie?"

An irritated expression appeared on Frankie's face.

Immediately, Anna gave a gushing smile to Frankie that knocked her off her guard. You could tell straight away that Frankie couldn't quite work out if Anna was actually being nice or nasty to her.

"Umm . . . errr . . . want?" Frankie asked.

"Yes," Anna continued to speak through her sickly sweet smile. "How can I help you? I'm just guessing you want to ask me for something. Otherwise, I don't suppose you'd be here, talking to me."

"Oh! Ha, ha, ha, ha," Frankie giggled nervously, and, like a troupe of trained circus poodles, the Franki-ettes joined her. "Oh, Anna, you are so funny! Of course I'd be here talking to you."

"So?" Anna said, her smile fading.

"Well, as I was saying," Frankie continued. "Your hair—it's always so gorgeous these days . . . Now that you work at the Cutting Room. I was, er, just wondering if they ever needed house models? For competitions and things?"

"Oh, I get it!" Anna said. "You read about Nicky entering the hairdressing competition in the local paper."

"Ummmm." Frankie hesitated and then said, "Well yes, actually now you mention it, I did spot it, I think."

"And you fancy being one of the models?"

"Well—I was just offering my services," Frankie explained. "I thought it might help the salon to have a professional model in their lineup when they enter the competition." The fixed smile appeared back on Frankie's face.

Anna leaned forward to her conspiratorially. "Ever so sorry, Frankie, but you're too late. We've appointed all our models already. Actually, Beth's one of them."

Instantly, Frankie's smile changed to a sneer. "Beth?" She looked like she had just been told she had dog poo on her shoe.

"Yeah—she's going to look gorgeous." Anna rubbed it in dramatically. "See ya!"

Anna gave Frankie and the others a dismissive wave and turned back round toward me, winking.

"Beth?" Frankie continued. "*Beth* is going to *model*? With *that* hair?"

"Oh, thanks!" I said, breaking my silence. "Glad you like it!"

"Well," Frankie said huffily, not remotely bothered about insulting my locks. "I didn't realize that it was an amateur competition."

"It isn't!" Anna said, turning round triumphantly. "And they don't need you in it. Good-bye!"

Frankie opened her mouth as if to speak but nothing came out. Then she snapped it shut and turned, steaming out of the hall with her gang behind her.

"Bloody cheek!" I spat.

"Ignore her—she's a pain in the bum," Anna said, picking up her fork and stabbing at a piece of bow-shaped pasta. "Oh, yuck!"

Anna's face was a picture of misery as she slowly chewed over what was in her mouth.

"Problem?" I couldn't help giggling at Anna's expression.

"Gross—it's cold!"

Having my hair done by Nicky was just fantastic. I could have let him play with it for hours. Actually, it *was* hours. Because I got to the salon at about six, and by nine, Nicky was still tweaking me about with gel and spray and Anna was still waiting attendance on him, when my phone rang.

I looked down at the screen. It was Joey! How cool was that to be having your hair done by a top hairdresser for free when your boyfriend calls you? Jamelia, eat your heart out!

"Hello!"

"Hi, Beth—how's your hair?"

"Er—great, thanks. But how did you know about it?"

Nicky gave me a wink as he flicked the comb some more.

"Anna told me, of course!"

I felt instantly stupid. "Oh yeah," I replied lamely.

"So when are you going to be finished?" Joey wanted to know.

"Dunno," I said. "I don't think it can be that long." I lowered my voice to a whisper because I didn't want to sound as if I was getting impatient with Nicky.

"Oh." Nicky grinned. "We'll be done in about fifteen minutes."

"Fifteen minutes." I smiled at both Nicky and Joey as I said it. "Why?"

"I just wanted to see what you look like," Joey said.

My heart gave a little flutter.

"So how about I walk you home?" he went on.

"Great! Thanks! See you later, then!"

"Bye!"

"You'll knock him dead," Nicky smiled, clearly realizing that I'd just been speaking to my boyfriend. "What do you think?"

Nicky gave my hair a last tweak and stood back, his comb still poised in one hand, scissors at the ready in the other.

I turned my head from side to side as Anna held

up a mirror at the back of me, letting me see my reflection in the huge mirror in front of me. I looked pretty damn good, if I say so myself.

My hair had been blow-dried to double its usual volume and my fringe—or what was left of the fringe I was growing out—had been teased into long ringlets that hung down on either side of my face.

"It looks great." Anna smiled. "Don't you think?"

I couldn't help the huge grin that spread across my own face. "I think it's just brilliant!" I said. "Thanks!" I enthused to Nicky.

"No—thank *you* for being so patient," Nicky said. "Hang on, I'm just going to take a couple of pictures so that I can remember exactly what we've done this week."

Nicky snapped at me from all angles with his phone. "Can you make it here again next week?"

"Sure," I said. This pampering bug was addictive and I was happy to have some more time being treated.

My eye caught the clock on the wall. "Stuff! I'd better give my mum a call or she'll be coming here to collect me as well."

"Was your mum coming?" Anna asked. "I wish I'd known! Then I could have told my mum that you'd be giving me a lift and she wouldn't have made Joey come to fetch me."

I blinked a few times as I absorbed what Anna had just said, but was saved from needing to reply when my mum answered the phone. I explained to her that Joey was going to walk me back with Anna and flipped my phone shut.

I felt humiliated and stupid. How dumb was I to think that Joey was making a special journey to see me, when all along he was really coming to pick Anna up anyway and I was just an add-on?

"Hello, love," Mum said when I walked into the living room. "Hey, your hair looks amazing."

"Oh, thanks," I replied, slumping down onto the sofa next to her. "Where is everyone?"

"Well, Jack's in bed," Mum explained. "He went to a party at Mungle Jungle after school today and he was exhausted. Anyway, it is a school night, remember?"

"Course," I said, feeling pretty wrecked myself. "What about Dad?"

"Oh, he's at some committee meeting at the cricket pavilion," Mum said. "Something to do with raising funds for repairs."

"Yawnsville," I sighed.

"Isn't it?" Mum giggled in agreement. "It was nice of Joey to bring you home—thank goodness he did or I'd have had a grumpy Jack in the car with me."

"Yeah."

"So you didn't want to ask him in, then? For coffee?" Mum said, trying to sound casual.

"No—Anna was with us."

"Oh," Mum replied. "But she could have come in as well."

"Yeah, but you know," I fudged. "It's a school night, like you say."

The truth was, I just wasn't in the mood for chatting with Joey and Anna. Yes, I was tired—trust me, having your hair played with is more tiring than you'd imagine—but actually I was still hacked off with Joey, knowing that he hadn't come to get me because he wanted to see me.

"I think I'm going to go up," I said.

"Beth, love?"

"Yeah?"

"Is everything okay? With you and Anna?"

"What do you mean?"

"You haven't had a row, have you?" Mum wanted to know. She'd hated it when Anna and I had ever fallen out when we were younger. She always went to elaborate lengths to make sure we made up ASAP and seemed to think that she was always personally responsible when we did, even though we would have anyway.

"Course not," I said. "Anna and I are great."

"So have you had a row with Joey, then?"

She wasn't going to give up.

"No, Mum, honestly. I told you, I'm tired. I'm off to bed. Night," I replied, walking quickly to the door.

"Well, as long as you're okay," she said.

"Course."

"Night then, love."

"Night."

"I am going to kebab that girl!" Anna steamed as she gave the evils to Frankie across the hall at lunchtime.

"Shall I light the charcoal for you?" I giggled. "What's she up to now?"

"She's only going to the seventies gig." Anna's eyes were wide with horror.

"No way!"

"Yes way!" Anna dug into her lunch with her fork (some kind of brown meat, sort of shaped, origin unknown). "All the Franki-ettes are going. Ugh, they're little maggots!"

"What, in your lunch?" I gagged on my soup (tomato, from a tin, so hopefully safe).

"What?" Anna puzzled.

"The maggots! Are they in the meat?"

"Gross! Where?" Anna threw her fork down in disgust. And so did everyone else who was on our and the surrounding tables.

"Your maggots," I insisted. "You said you found maggots in your food."

"No, I didn't," Anna said, indignantly. "I said Frankie and her cheerleaders were little maggots."

"Sorry?"

"For worming their way to the seventies gig," Anna explained.

"Oh, I see what you mean!" I giggled, suddenly realizing. "But how do you know? About them coming to the gig?"

"Oh, it's no good," Anna said, shoving her plate away. "It's so vile even maggots wouldn't eat it."

"Here," I said, passing her my roll. "Have this and tell me how you know about Dusterbrain coming to the gig."

"Thanks." Anna grabbed the roll and pulled a chunk out of it. "I heard her blabbing about it in maths."

Maths was one of the only subjects that Anna and I didn't do together because we're in different classes.

"Well, there'll be loads of people there," I pacified. "You probably won't even see her."

"Oh, as if!" Anna wailed. "She's going to be wearing a bright pink satin catsuit. How could I miss that?"

"I take your point," I commiserated. "A bright pink satin catsuit? Blimey, no one will miss her! Listen, you are going to be looking so stunning in those hot pants and boots you won't have time to care."

"Too right," Anna said, sitting up straight.

"You," I said pointedly, "are going to make everyone look at *you*, girl!"

Going round to Anna's was a real laugh on the Friday night. Anna's mum had found some amazing clothes for her to wear.

"I cannot believe your mum wore these," I declared, holding up a pair of shiny plastic shorts.

"Actually, she didn't, they belonged to my aunt, who's even older than my mum," Anna explained. "You know, the one who lives in Canada?"

"So how come your mum's got them?" I asked.

"Oh, my gran kept loads of stuff," Anna said, pulling on a blue-and-white striped halter top. "She made this, apparently—knitted it. . . ."

"Very ABBA," I said.

"And if you can believe it," Anna continued, "these boots were Gran's!"

She held up a pair of long white boots that had the highest white platforms I have ever seen.

"No way!" I exclaimed. "How could your gran walk in these?"

"Dunno, but she did, because Mum said she used to meet them from the school bus stop in them. Cool, eh?"

"Ace." I nodded approvingly.

Once Anna was dressed, we crimped her hair so that it looked completely crazy and wild. Then I set to with some double-sparkly blue eye shadow, lots of eyeliner, and some super-over-the-top mascara that made Anna's eyes look like enormous spiders had given up their legs for her. I finished her seventies look off with some pale lip gloss that was so shiny I could almost see my reflection in it.

"Wow!" Anna exclaimed when she saw herself in the mirror. "Waterloo! Thanks, Beth. I really wish you were coming too. . . ."

But before I had the chance to answer, the door-bell rang and Sam had come to get her.

"Not bad," said Joey, coming out of the living room to see what all the fuss was about. "Not good, either, but not bad."

"Oh, bog off," Anna said.

"Wow!" Sam exclaimed as he stood at the bottom

of the stairs in his outrageously flared jeans and a satin bomber jacket.

"Where did you get that outfit?" Anna wondered.

"From the fancy dress shop," Sam said, clearly pleased with himself. "Gorgeous, aren't I?"

"Modest, too!" I giggled. "Can you walk in those boots?"

They were red patents with platforms almost as big as the number of hits from ABBA.

"Actually, they're shoes," Sam explained, pulling up his flares to reveal some staggeringly bright socks and some fluorescent yellow laces.

"Omigod—you need prescription sunglasses just to look at them," Joey yelled, covering his eyes with his arms. "And a license to go out dressed like that. You cannot be serious."

"And your point is?" Anna demanded.

"That you two surely don't want to be seen in public like that," Joey stated.

"They look great," I said honestly. "Sensational, even."

"Precisely," agreed Sam.

"Exactly," confirmed Anna.

"Absolutely," I said, in case there was any doubt remaining.

"A pair of umbrellas, if you ask me," Joey declared.

"I don't think anyone did," Anna snapped. "Come on, we're off."

"Have a groovy time!" I grinned, taking a picture of them with my phone.

"We will," said Sam, putting his arm around Anna's shoulder.

"If we don't break our ankles before we even get there," giggled Anna, stepping gingerly down the front step.

"Give Frankie a kick from me," I suggested, blowing Anna a kiss.

And they were off.

"They look like Tellytubbies crossed with Ronald McDonald crossed with a pair of clowns." Joey smirked. "Fancy going out like that."

"Yeah," I half giggled.

Why was he so against them going off and having fun at the gig? I wondered. And why was I agreeing with him instead of saying what I thought?

"Fancy a quick game on the Xbox?" Joey suggested. "Then you can help me clean my football boots."

"Er, sure," I croaked. He slid his hand into mine and I decided that even cleaning football boots with Joey might be fun. A great alternative to being at a gig, eh?

☺

I met up with Anna again at lunchtime on Saturday.

"Tell me, tell me," I said, gathering my knees to my chest and tucking into my tuna sandwich.

"It was a-mazing," Anna stated dramatically. "The band was brilliant, they were called Waterloo, and it was like everyone knew all the words to all the sounds. But then we were helped by the words being on a kind of karaoke machine."

"Fantastic," I said.

"I've decided my eighteenth birthday party has to be a seventies night," Anna went on. "I tell you it was mega."

"And did you see Frankie?" I wondered.

"Sadly, yes," Anna said. "But I could tell she was knocked out by my outfit. Green, even. Anyway—who cares?"

I was glad that Frankie hadn't got up Anna's nose.

"My feet are absolutely killing me, though," Anna said, shoving off her supermarket-fake Birkenstocks, and rubbing her toes. "I wish I could wash people's hair sitting down."

"So go on—tell me more," I nudged. "I need to know far more detail than that."

And Anna obliged. She filled me in on everything, all the seventies hits and what other people were wearing. The fact that Frankie had not been at the gig with her boyfriend made us speculate that she had split up with him. Apparently, all the Franki-ettes had been wearing outfits almost identical to Frankie's. And most important, Anna and Sam had obviously had a brilliant time.

"I tell you, Beth—I am whacked."

"You must be," I commiserated.

"So what did you two get up to last night?" Anna wanted to know.

"Me and Joey?"

"No, you and your pet hamster. Of course Joey!"

"Oh, Xbox, you know," I muttered, shoving my sandwich quickly into my mouth.

"Xbox—that's it?"

"No," I said.

"So? What else?"

"Well—I helped Joey get his kit ready for football this evening," I defended. Joey and Sam had a flood-lit match that evening.

"You ironed Joey's kit with him?" Anna said in disbelief.

"No way! I just helped him with his boots."

"You what?" Anna turned and gaped at me, square on. "You cleaned his boots? His smelly, muddy football boots?"

"I only did one of them," I snapped. "Joey did the other one himself."

"I don't believe my brother got you to clean his boots for him," Anna wailed. "And I don't believe you did it! Beth—for God's sake! What kind of a Friday night was that?"

A boring one, I thought. But I wasn't going to admit it to Anna.

"Well, we had to save our cash for tomorrow," I lied, although it was, I suppose, true in a way. "For the London Dungeons."

"Oh, sure," Anna said, almost as if she believed me, but with a sideways look in her eye.

"Come on, eat up," I urged. "I'm suffering from Gross Retail Deprivation. I want to go to Accessorize."

"How can you suffer from GRD?" Anna wailed, wincing as she squeezed her toes back into her shoes. "You work in a shop!"

"It's a supermarket, okay? It does nothing for my GRD."

"Okay, but you said you're saving your cash for

Sunday." For someone so tired, Anna wasn't giving up easily.

"I can look, can't I? Come on!"

It had finally arrived: Sunday. The day that we were going to the London Dungeons.

Sam and Joey were excited before we'd even got on the train, and carried on laughing and giggling all the way to London Bridge. They were like little kids. They talked about a football match that had taken place, live, last night. They had actually played football and then gone home to watch even more football on the telly.

For some strange reason, they both thought it was extraordinary that neither Anna nor I had bothered to watch it, preferring to see a TV movie on another channel. Actually, Sam and Joey had us in fits of laughter when they were talking about the referee and some of the dodgy decisions he'd made. I don't know how they managed to make the most boring things sound so amusing.

"Hey, look," Joey said, excitedly standing up and grabbing his coat. "Get all your stuff. We're here!"

His sense of urgency was contagious and we all sprang to attention as the train pulled in to the platform.

It was like Follow the Leader as we tripped along behind Joey and Sam. Before we knew it, we were standing on a huge concourse surrounded by people with enormous rucksacks and suitcases, all of them waiting or reading the announcements of arrivals and departures.

"Where do we go from here?" I asked.

"Dunno," Joey said. "I'd have thought they would signpost the way into the Dungeons."

"It said on the website that you just walked out of the station and down the steps," Anna said helpfully.

"So where is it, then?" Sam was getting a bit cross, and I was with him. It was much colder here than it was on the train. Freezing, in fact. Anyway, if we were going to get spooked out of our lives, I wanted to get in there and just get it over with.

"Well, there must be a sign," I said matter-of-factly. After all, there were signs for everything else. I spun around in a circle, taking the place in.

"There!" Sam called. "Those doors there."

So we all followed him out and clumped down the stairs.

"Oh!"

"You're kidding!"

At the bottom of the stairs, we were met with a huge, long snaked queue of people. Our eyes followed the line to its beginning—which was just underneath a burning torch that lit up a sign saying LONDON DUNGEONS.

"No way!" I sighed, wondering how long we were going to be standing in the street before we got in.

"Blimey, I bet it takes him a while to put his makeup on in the morning." I nodded toward some bloke who was dressed up like the Grim Reaper, with a trailing black cloak and a long scythe in his gnarled, long-nailed hands. He sneered at me in acknowledgment as he walked on down the queue.

"I never thought there'd be this many people on a Sunday," Anna giggled, linking her arm through mine as we joined the back of the queue. "Oh well, it can't take that long to get in."

Joey and Sam bounced up behind us. "Boo!" Joey said.

"Jeez, it's so flipping cold," grumbled Sam.

"Group hug to stay warm," Joey announced, and Anna and I found ourselves as the jam in the sandwich, being squeezed breathless. At least it kept out the chilly wind.

We looked back to see that even more people had already joined the queue behind us.

"How dare so many people turn up on the same day as us," Anna declared.

"Do you think we should go up there and tell them all that Beth is an important member of the royal family and they should allow us VIP access IMMEDIATELY?" Joey asked, rather loudly. So loudly that people had turned round to see who was making all the noise. I could feel my cheeks burning but Anna seemed to be taking it all in her stride. How come she could do that and I couldn't? All the messing about was just making me even more nervous about what horrors awaited us inside.

"Please!" I begged. "Don't!"

"Let's play girlfriend-twirling!" Sam said, scooping Anna up and tossing her over his shoulder. "It's a simple game and it might pass the time a bit faster. See how fast you can go before she pukes!"

"Put me down, you nutter!" Anna giggled, but sounding for all the world as if the last thing she actually wanted was for Sam to let go of her.

I couldn't help giggling because Anna's laughter was infectious. Sam started slowly turning round. He obviously wasn't trying to make her ill; besides, he was having to be careful not to take out other people in the queue, although most of them were giving us a pretty wide berth as it was.

"You're on!" Joey took up the challenge and before I knew it, he was picking me up and, with a loud groaning noise, trying to shove me onto his shoulder.

"Don't drop me!" I called, laughing but also terri-fied that he would. I was so glad that I was wearing jeans and not a skirt that would show the whole of London Bridge's inhabitants my knickers.

"Grrnnnt," Joey moaned as he gave another heave to try and toss me higher over his shoulder. My stomach was really beginning to hurt and this suddenly didn't seem very funny anymore.

"Put me down!" I pleaded. "Now!"

With another grunt, Joey did, and I tumbled to the floor, not remotely gracefully, my jacket all around my ears. My face red from being upside down. I felt dizzy from being turned upside down and looked at Anna, who had been far more courteously lowered by Sam.

"Cor—my back," Joey moaned loudly, rubbing it. "Blimey, you're heavy, Beth."

Oh great, thanks, I thought. Who needs horrible people like Frankie in the world when your own boyfriend makes you feel rubbish so easily?

"More like you're too weak to lift her!" Anna spluttered. "Come on—the queue's moving on."

Chapter Seven

Is Your Boyfriend Your Best Friend?

It was another cold hour before we actually got to the entrance to the Dungeons. A long cold hour, during which Joey gave a ceaseless entertainment of conversation and larking about.

Despite the cold, the Joey and Sam sideshow was quite funny—at first. But after a while, I began to wonder how much more I could laugh. I mean, my cheekbones were beginning to hurt. And I was beginning to find the twenty-four/seven jokes not so funny. Anna didn't seem to be having quite such a problem with it. She seemed to be enjoying it, even. What was my problem?

Then, just as I thought we'd made it in, we realized that we still had to queue some more to actually get to pay for our tickets.

"Do you think these are real gravestones?" Sam wanted to know.

"As if!" Anna said sarcastically. "Yes, they just popped out to the gravestone supermarket and bought some. Give over, you moron!"

"What?" Sam said, his eyes wide and innocent.

"The skeletons could be, though," Joey added. "I mean, grave-robbery was all the rage at one point."

"Used to be," I pointed out. "It's hardly a modern crime statistic that they talk about on *Crimewatch*."

Anna and I giggled and rubbed our arms to keep a bit warmer.

"Oh, ha, ha." Joey folded his arms dramatically. "But, Miss Clever Clogs, once upon a time grave-robbery was a big thing."

"Meaning?" Anna wanted to know.

"Meaning that there must have been a lot of bones left over from then. You know."

Anna and I looked at each other blankly. What was Joey on about?

"So come on then, Einstein," Sam said, clearly not having any more idea of what Joey was talking about than Anna or I did. Which was a relief. "So what's this leading to?"

Joey looked back at us all and shook his head. "Well, it's obvious, isn't it? They must have had a lot of bones left over from when they were catching the robbers."

"And? Your point is?" Sam interrogated, raising his eyebrows in puzzlement.

Anna and I just looked at each other and raised ours in agreement.

"And so maybe the leftover bones are the ones they've used here!" Joey said, exasperated.

"Ohhhh—no way!" I groaned. "They must be plastic, surely?"

"You are just sick!" Anna said, playfully whacking her brother on his shoulder.

"What did I say?" Joey said innocently.

"Pack it in, mate," Sam said. "Come on—the queue's moving on at last."

The queue meandered slowly round the corner to what we hoped was the ticket booth, but it was then that we realized we had to have our photo taken before we got there.

"Oh yes!" Sam exclaimed. "Now we're talking!"

"Okay," the photographer said. "So, we could have the girls in the prison at the back, screaming for the boys as one of them has his head chopped off and the other is the axe man!"

This was clearly a man who loved his job.

"Come on." I grabbed Anna's arm and we bundled to the prison at the back and peered through the grating. "Let's look like pathetic girls who are screaming for their hunter-gatherers!"

I giggled at the thought of Joey and Sam being either interested in or capable of protecting us. And laughed even more at the thought of wanting to be looked after by them.

"Do you think there are rats in here?" Anna wondered, looking sheepishly to her feet.

I was glad she was as freaked by this place as I had been.

"God, I hope not!" I shuffled from one foot to the other. I'd put the rats-thought out of my head, but now I was reminded it made me feel all squeamish again.

"Get your chopper out, then, Sam!" Joey said exceptionally loudly, and laughed helplessly at his own joke.

"I will, mate," Sam agreed enthusiastically.

We took our positions behind the grille of our prison.

"Little boys, eh?" I whispered to Anna, and we rolled our eyes.

From behind Joey and Sam, I could see a group of girls further back in the queue. They were laughing appreciatively at Sam and Joey and I got the distinct impression that they fancied them.

"Did you see them?" I hissed at Anna through my cheek-ache grin for the camera.

But before she had a chance to answer, the photographer said, "Okay—scream!" and the moment for answering was lost.

"Aaaaaaaaagh!"

"Beth—you all right?" Anna said, leaning down toward me.

Actually, I was gagging too much on the smell of the festering human-waste pit on the other side of the room to be able to reply.

"Ohhh . . ." I started to retch again. Why wasn't anyone else having this problem? Truly, the smell was just revolting. And trust me to be the pathetic one who couldn't ignore it.

"What's the problem?" Joey asked. "It's not real poo, Beth! It's just pretend."

Even from my vulnerable, almost upside down position in the corner, I could sense that Joey's big mouth was making the other visitors to the Dungeons turn around and gape at me. Great. Terrific. That was just what I needed.

"You all right?" Sam asked, sounding far more concerned than Joey.

"She's just feeling a bit hot, that's all," Anna said in my defense as I tried to wipe my hair from my eyes.

I grabbed a tissue from my pocket and wiped the tears from my eyes, realizing as I did that my makeup had probably smudged all over my face. This was just getting so much better by the minute.

"Come on, Beth," Joey said. "It's just a laugh. I mean, it's only pretend!" He giggled. I wasn't entirely sure if he was laughing at me or trying to cheer me up.

I drew myself up and pushed my hair back and blew my nose.

"I'm absolutely fine," I lied. "Come on—let's move on to the next room."

Joey and Sam positively skipped into the next chamber, only hesitating for a few seconds to say, "Wow—come and see these neck stretchers! He-he!"

"Obviously the torture chamber." I smiled weakly at Anna.

Anna smirked back and asked, "You feeling any better?"

"Sure—but God, did it honk back there! How come you could handle it?"

"Because I live with Joey and his feet are even worse than that stench in there!"

I did a real belly laugh then and felt loads better immediately.

"Anna—is my makeup okay?"

"Can I ask the audience?"

"Please—no," I replied firmly. "They've had enough entertainment out of me today."

"Well—better wipe away that smudge under your left eye or you might look like a candidate for Frankenstein's sister." Anna wiped the smut away. "That's better."

She put her arm through mine and led me on through the doors. "Come on—we don't want to look like lightweights who can't cope with a bit of impaling, do we?"

Actually, the London Dungeons—save for the quite revolting stench—was brilliant.

Thankfully, the rats were kept well in control behind a huge window so that you could watch them running riot behind the glass. They looked quite clean and healthy—I'm sure they were a lot more appealing than a real plague rat. There was one room we went in and were told all about Jack the Ripper and his victims. Now, that *was* creepy and made the hairs stand on the back of your neck. I didn't much like the photographs of the victims that they showed us, either. On the slab. Dead. Lovely.

As you moved from place to place in the dark, it was difficult, sometimes impossible, to work out what was a mannequin and who was a real person. If Anna and I hadn't jumped out of our skins when a suit of armor jumped out on Sam and Joey, causing *them* to scream loudly (for a change), I think we would have enjoyed the fact that Joey and Sam had been finally caught out. Hah!

I began to wonder if the staff at the Dungeons had sent word ahead about the pair of idiots, namely Joey and Sam, who were visiting the place that day, because as soon as we entered the courtroom, the judge shoved the pair of them in the dock to sentence them.

Of course Sam and Joey loved the attention and played up to their performance beautifully. Everyone was laughing uproariously and even Anna and I had to admit that they'd done pretty well.

But finally, we found ourselves on the way to the exit. It wasn't as straightforward as it sounds, though, as we were now walking through the Fire of London. Not real flames lashing at our feet, of course, but pretty scary all the same.

"What's the holdup?" Anna wondered as the

queue of people in front of us came to a standstill.

"Search me," I replied, straining to see over the heads in front of us.

You could just about make out a couple of women who were hesitating ahead of us.

"What's happening?" All the flames and darkness were beginning to get me nervous again.

"Who knows?" Anna smiled slightly at me. "But I'm sure we'll be okay."

"Course," I said, shuffling slowly ahead in the queue.

We were being funneled through this corridor that led us into a kind of rotating chamber so that the "flames" were whipping around us, going over our heads and under our feet.

"Omigod!" Anna said as she stepped into the room of fire. Actually, I should say "stopped," not "stepped," because she positively froze and grabbed the handrails.

I landed with a thud on the walkway behind her.

"Woooaaah!" I breathed.

It was awful and amazing. As the room seemed to spin around, it was impossible to know where your feet were landing. It was as if your legs had turned to jelly and your feet no longer existed. And all the while, these "flames" were menacingly licking over your head.

"Come on, you two!" Joey prodded impatiently in my back. "There's a queue here!"

"We know that," I hissed under my breath.

"You okay, Anna?" Sam asked, peering over our heads. At least he sounded like he actually wanted to know. Unlike Joey, who didn't seem to care about either of us.

"Sure," Anna replied unconvincingly. Then she turned to me and said, "I think I'm just about to rainbow cake. Stop the world—please?"

"Excuse me," Joey said, shoving past us and into the tunnel. "Oh!"

He slowed up—in fact, he almost stopped. Ha!

"Oh, this is easy," he said, not sounding quite as confident as before and grabbing firmly on to the handrails with both hands. He moved ahead a bit sheepishly at first, looking around him and making a distinct wobble with his legs. "All you have to do is hold on to the rails and look down on the floor!" And he was gone.

"What?" Anna said, looking back at me and looking uneasily at the by now very long queue of people behind us who hadn't even yet gotten the chance to discover quite how awful this final experience was.

"Come on—let's just try it and get out of here," I said, gently nudging Anna to move on. To be honest, I was feeling a little pleased that for once it was Anna rather than me who was freaking out.

"Okay," she said. "Head down and here I go!"

On the one hand, I was pleased to be well rid of that horrible tunnel. On the other hand, it was very annoying that Joey was quite so smug about how he'd worked it out and the rest of us hadn't.

I was glad that he didn't go on about it for long because now we were in the shop, Joey was having a great time with Sam, playing with a pen that looked like a hideous severed finger. Instead of blue ink, it oozed a kind of blood-red goo. All this blood, gore, and horribleness was beginning to wear a bit thin for both me and Anna.

"Oh, for God's sake, you two!" Anna pulled a face and covered her nose as the most revolting bodily function noise emitted from where Sam and Joey were standing. She and I moved back to distance ourselves. "Can't you at least wait until you get outside?"

"What?" Joey said, smiling sweetly at us. Then he dramatically took the severed finger and pulled the top back off again, allowing the pen to exhale the same farting noise we'd just heard.

"Gotcha!" Sam laughed, and Anna and I had to giggle with him.

Joey, unfortunately, had to keep making the finger-farting noises for ages. Until even the shop assistant asked him if he was actually going to buy the pen and, if not, would he please leave it alone?

The shop was stuffed with gross things, and in the end I bought a ball that was a wobbling bloodshot eyeball for my brother, Jack. Normally, I wouldn't buy anything for Jack, but with Sam and Joey buying things so enthusiastically, I kind of felt that I had to look willing and buy something.

"Right, then," Sam said as we left the Dungeons. "Who's for a McDonald's with loads of bloody tomato sauce oozing from it?"

"Hardy-har!" Anna giggled and put her arm through his.

"What did I say?" he asked innocently as we headed for something to eat.

Joey and I walked along behind them. I didn't know how Joey would react if I put my arm through his. But I didn't want to try in case he didn't want me to. After all, I noticed that he hadn't put his arm through mine. You see? There I was again, wondering how things *should* be, rather than just getting on with it.

Chapter Eight
Has He Told You He Loves You?

"Nice day, love?"

When I walked into the living room, Dad was fast asleep on the sofa and Mum was watching a repeat of *Midsomer Murders*. Jack was playing some kind of bloodcurdling computer game in the corner.

"Okay, thanks." I couldn't work out if I was lying or not. To be honest, the day had left me feeling a bit rubbish.

"What were the Dungeons like?" Mum wanted to know. "I've been thinking that maybe we'd take Jack for his birthday."

My brother just sat at his computer game,

completely ignoring me and oblivious to the fact that Mum was talking about him.

"Loud," I explained, thinking of all those banging doors and bloodcurdling screams. "Dark. Smelly, too."

"Smelly?" Mum scrunched her nose up in disgust. "Why smelly?"

"Oh—you know," I explained. "Stinky plague pits, loads of poo. That sort of stuff. Jack would love it. You should take him." *Lose him there, even,* I thought wickedly.

"I'm glad you had a good time," Mum said.

"Mmmm," I sighed. "Fancy something to drink?"

"Actually, I was just going to make some tea," Mum said, putting down the magazine that she was half reading. "Why don't you pop the kettle on and I'll make it?"

"Well, I was just going to go up and finish off some homework." I was definitely lying now.

"I'll bring something up for you, then." Mum smiled.

"Thanks."

It was about ten minutes later that Mum knocked on my bedroom door and came in, not just with a drink, but a piece of quite scrummy-looking cake on a plate.

"What's this?" I asked. "Who made it?"

"I did," Mum said defensively.

"But you never make cakes!" I exclaimed.

"I don't *often* make cakes, I agree," Mum commented. "But I won't if you don't want me to."

"Certainly looks good," I said, taking the plate and mug from Mum and putting them on my desk. I didn't sit down on my bed because, to be honest, I didn't really want my mum to think I was wanting her to sit down with me for a chat. I didn't want a chat—with her or anybody. I just wanted to have a think about what was bothering me.

I switched on my computer.

"I'll let you get on with it, then," Mum said, turning back toward the door and getting the hint.

"Thanks." I sat down at my desk.

"Beth? Are you sure you're okay?"

"Course," I snapped, not looking up at her and instead staring resolutely at my screen.

"It's just that you seem a bit down after your day out."

"Honestly, I'm just tired, that's all. It's been a busy weekend, what with work and all." I clicked away with my mouse. "And I really need to catch up with my homework."

"Yes," Mum said. "As long as you're all right, then."

"I'll see you later, then," I muttered. "And thanks for the cake, Mum."

"Pleasure." And she shut the door.

I instantly stopped fiddling with my computer— I'd already seen that there was nothing in my inbox anyway—and waited until I could hear that my mum had gone downstairs and back into the living room.

I slurped at my drink and then stuffed some of the cake in my mouth. It was good—very good. I quickly scoffed the lot and then flung myself onto my bed.

My mum wanted to know had I enjoyed my day. So had I? Well, I was glad that I'd actually gone to the Dungeons because it was somewhere I'd heard loads about. But honestly, had I really enjoyed it? I didn't really know. I mean, yes, it was interesting. And yes, it was a bit of a laugh—some of the time. And yet . . . I hadn't come home feeling like I'd had a good day. Instead, I'd come home feeling a bit fed up.

I mean, normally when I'd been somewhere with Anna, I'd come home feeling up about it—except school, of course. We'd have a giggle on the journey home and then hang out together afterward, talking about what we'd been doing and who we'd been doing it with or who we'd seen there. In other words, a jolly good gossip.

Maybe that was my problem, then? The fact that I'd come back home on my own because Anna had gone back with Sam and Joey because Sam and Joey were going to watch some sports thing on Sky. Another sports thing. Lovely.

Obviously, I was missing my goss sesh with Anna. I leaned over and grabbed my copy of *Get It!* from the floor. I didn't even need to flip through the pages to find the famous quiz because it was already folded back in the right place. I didn't even need to bother with how often he sent me a text because it was basically hardly ever. But the second question, "How often do you see him?" I felt a bit better about. After all, I'd seen Joey twice this week. So no complaining there. Obviously, Joey was not, repeat NOT, into nicknames, and I knew that my idea of a perfect date was snuggling up in the cinema. I also knew that Joey did not think that was his idea of a perfect date. But then what, I was still trying to work out, was? I glanced down at the options:

a) snuggling up in the back seat of the cinema

b) A candlelit dinner for two somewhere expensive—and he's paying

c) Watching football from the side of the pitch
d) Watching football on the telly

Well, definitely not *a,* then. And he was not, so far, anyway, the sort of person who gave the impression that a romantic dinner at his expense was something he was going to volunteer for.

I reckoned that either *c* or *d* would be something for him. Unfortunately, though, it wasn't for me.

Question six was one I would really rather have avoided:

Is he a grown-up or a groan-up?
a) His favorite thing is a whoopee cushion
b) His favorite thing is his MP3 player
c) His favorite thing is his dog
d) His favorite thing is his teddy bear

I doubted very much that Joey had a teddy bear. Maybe I was wrong, but I just couldn't see him as being sentimental enough to keep his childhood teddy. It probably isn't really a boy thing.

Anna's mum was allergic to cats and dogs, so there wasn't a pet in Joey's house, so I couldn't go for that option. But if I thought about it, I could kind of imagine Joey as being one of those people who went off to the park with some huge hairy dog with a cute face that spent hours and hours retrieving a stick or a ball. So maybe that was the right answer?

On the other hand, Joey loved gadgets and computers. And if I was answering that question about me, I'd be tempted to say that I loved my MP3 myself. But then there was the whoopee cushion option. After a day with Sam and Joey, turning me and Anna upside down, all that talk about choppers and neck stretchers, all that leaping about and joking about rats, the whoopee cushion option suddenly seemed like a goer.

Joey hardly took things seriously, did he? He was not into worrying about what other people thought about him. Yes, he would probably love to have a whoopee cushion. In fact, if I thought about it, I bet he already owned one. I sighed and took another slug of my drink.

Anyway, who wanted a boyfriend who was dull, boring, and snotty? Having a boyfriend who was up for a laugh was much better.

So question seven was next: "Is your boyfriend your best friend?" Well, obviously not. But that was because I had the *best* best friend that anyone could ever want with Anna. But I glanced down the list of answers to that question:

a) You could tell him your darkest secret and he'd keep it
b) He's always ready to hug you when you cry
c) He spends as much time with the lads as with you
d) You'd never tell him when you were fed up about something

Could I tell Joey my darkest secret? Well—would I want to? To be fair to Joey, I'd always confide in Anna. Always. But hypothetically, if I did confide in Joey, I wondered—would he keep the secret?

Difficult one. But then I thought about the way Joey was with Sam, and I couldn't help but think that Joey would probably blab to Sam about stuff. So no, I reckoned I wouldn't tell him my darkest secret, even if I hadn't told Anna, because I wouldn't trust Joey not to split on me.

But would Joey give me a hug when I was upset? Before I'd started going out with Joey, I would have said a definite yes to that one. And then, if I thought back to earlier that day, Joey was happy to leap into Sam's group hug. He'd also asked if I was all right when I was feeling ill. But he wasn't that convincing about being worried about me—I mean *really* worried about me. More like he was irritated that I was holding everyone up.

Honest answer? I wasn't at all sure what Joey would do if he saw me cry. It might depend on the mood he was in as much as my own. *C* was obviously going to be a yes—because Joey spent at least as much time with his mates as he did with me. Truthfully, I knew he spent more because I wasn't convinced that he spent hours sitting at home studying or surfing the Net. He was one of those lucky people who did well with the minimum of work. Anyway, I would never tell him that I was fed up about something. Because I just knew that he wouldn't be interested. But then, what boyfriend would?

Question eight made me feel sick: "Has he told you he loves you?" Well, definitely not *a*, which was yes. I wondered if Sam had told Anna that he loved her—probably not, because I imagine Anna would just laugh if someone told her that. Anna was out for a laugh—she wasn't some wet romantic heroine.

I supposed that *b* was the answer for me because

no, Joey had most definitely not told me he loved me. But then maybe it was *c* because I went out with Joey for a giggle. Could I honestly say that, though? I mean, Joey had been just so irritating today.

Perhaps, though, my answer was *d,* I didn't love him? *Did* I love him? How should I know? . . . This boyfriend lark was such hard work.

I told Jack all about the London Dungeons over supper that night. He was definitely up for it when Mum said she was going to take him for his birthday.

Of course, I didn't mention anything about almost puking at the smells and being terrified out of my wits by the wall of fire and the Jack the Ripper bit. But I did play up all the gory bits and the torture chambers. Right up my baby brother's street.

After watching something really corny on the telly, I had a bath and went to bed. Slipping into bed, I checked my phone to see if Anna had sent me a message. She hadn't. But there was one from Joey.

Bn thnkng bout stff. Thnk we shld cOl it.

Was he dumping me?

Chapter Nine

Would You Rather Have a Date with Your Mate than with Your Boy?

I looked at the screen on my phone again and again and again. Had I made a mistake and read it the wrong way? Had I really been dumped? Had he really dumped me by text and not even had enough courage—not to say decency—to ring me and tell me? Or tell me in person?

I felt humiliated, angry, and—I am ashamed to say—like crying. Here was me wondering whether I really enjoyed being with Joey and he'd gone and dumped me before I got the chance to do anything about it!

And another thing: Was I meant to reply to his message? If I did, though, what would I say to him? Thnx—hd a grt tIm 2day. C U arnd? Or maybe Get

Stffd! I chucked my phone back onto my desk and slunk back on my bed. I lay there for God knows how long, just looking at the ceiling, Joey's text message going round and round in my head.

After a while, my head started throbbing and I realized that my mouth was pinched together and I was clenching my teeth.

I punched the duvet beneath me in frustration that I was being so pathetic about a stupid text message from a stupid boy. And then, without being able to stop them, hot stinging tears started to pour down my face. I rolled over and sobbed into the pillow.

I don't know how long I lay there but I was taken by surprise when there was a gentle tap on my door and Mum slipped in.

"Beth—are you asleep?"

For a few seconds, I wondered if I could blag it and not answer.

"Beth? Love?"

Mum sat down on my bed.

"Hi," I said, blinking.

"Can I turn the light on?" But before I could answer, Mum already had. "Oh—sorry," Mum apologized as I blinked at the brightness.

I could tell immediately that she knew I'd been crying, but she didn't mention it. Not directly.

"Is everything all right, Beth? Only you seemed a bit down at supper."

"Oh—I'm okay. I said I was."

"I know you said you were, Beth," Mum said gently. "But I'm not convinced."

I didn't say anything. Nor did Mum for a moment or two.

"Was Joey with you today?"

"Mmm."

"Only you don't always seem to be that happy when you've seen Joey these days."

I said nothing. I just didn't know what to say. I wasn't sure if I wanted to tell her that I thought he'd dumped me. I didn't want to tell her that, after waiting for what seemed like ages to actually have a boyfriend, I'd finally got one and was wondering what all the fuss had been about. That boys seemed to be a bit . . . a bit kind of irritating, really.

Mum looked at me and stroked a stray piece of hair off my forehead.

"If you ask me, boyfriends are a pain," she said.

"Sorry?"

"Boyfriends," Mum said. "I used to spend hours wondering about what was going on in my boyfriends' heads. Did they like my hair? Was I saying the right thing? Was I being funny? Was I funny enough?"

"You did?"

My mum had lots of boyfriends before she met my dad? This was news to me.

"I had a few when I was at college." Mum grinned with a slightly knowing look, obviously reading my thoughts. I still didn't know what to say. Mum stroked my hair again. It felt nice. Soothing.

"What I learned in the end, though," Mum said after a while, "was that it didn't really matter what the boyfriends thought. It was how *I* felt—what *I* thought that mattered. I was fed up with sitting around waiting to see what they were going to suggest we did. I wanted to do my things sometimes. And sometimes I just wanted to hang out with my own friends."

"Sure," I said.

"Anyway." Mum kissed me on the head. "I'll leave you to sleep. Don't lie there worrying about things. Night, love."

"Night, Mum," I replied. "And thanks."

"No problem. Anytime."

And she was gone. How, I wondered, had Mum known? Without me even saying much, either. Wow. Mum.

@

The next morning, I switched on my phone and checked in my inbox. Maybe I'd misread Joey's message. Maybe he'd sent me another one saying it was only a joke. I hadn't. He hadn't.

With a kind of painful lump in my throat, I switched the phone off again. It was just all too humiliating. How could I look anyone in the eye at school?

I managed to avoid seeing Anna on the bus by cadging a lift with Dad. Normally, I'd do anything to get out of being in the car with Dad and having to listen to Terry Wogan on Radio Two.

As my dad laughed at the lame jokes on the radio, I tried to work out how I could face Anna. I mean, did she know that Joey had told me where to get off? If she did, was she going to be on his side?

It suddenly dawned on me that maybe I hadn't just lost my boyfriend, but my best friend as well. The lump in my throat hurt even more. I looked out of Dad's car window to the street. As if my mood wasn't gray enough, it was drizzling with rain, and I realized that this thing with Joey was about as difficult and complicated as I could imagine it could get when you finished with your boyfriend. When your boyfriend has dumped *you*.

When Dad dropped me off at the school gate, I checked my watch. I had about ten minutes to go before the assembly bell. If I got it right, I reckoned that I would be able to hang around in the school library for a while before I could slip into assembly at the back.

That way, I wouldn't get into trouble for being late and I'd be able to avoid Anna.

My plan worked. There was no one in the school library at that time of day except for Miss Mathias the librarian. When I walked in, she looked up, delighted that someone was swotty enough to use the place at that time of day.

I smiled back weakly and zoomed over to the art section, pretending that I was looking for something. Actually, I surprised myself by finding a book that would actually help me with some project work I was doing for D&T, so I ended up taking the book out. Poor old Miss Mathias looked like all her birthdays had come at once. I guess it made a difference from most of the kids who came in, who were usually in for detention.

"That is such a brilliant book," she said enthusiastically. "You're only the second person to borrow it. You'll love it."

"Thanks," I said just as the assembly bell went.

"Better go," I muttered, picking up the book and shoving it in my bag.

As I got to the bottom, I could see the usual crowd of noisy kids funneling into the hall. I just about made out Anna's head as she slipped in through the door. Phew.

I held back until the crowd filtered into a few stragglers like me, and slid in at the back of the room as everyone else was sitting down. Mrs. Pilgrim, my head of year, gave me a scowl of disapproval and poked pointedly at her watch with her finger. Equally pointedly, I indicated at the library book that was sticking out of my bag. Her scowl relaxed into a nod of approval and she pointed to the chair next to her at the end of the row. So it looked like the payback of trying to avoid Anna was to sit next to a teacher. Oh well.

From my seat I quickly got to see why the teachers always put themselves in such a place, because you could see what everyone was up to. Including Anna, who was looking all around her, anxiously.

Once I got into my first lesson, though, things got a bit trickier.

"Hey, Beth," Anna hissed, beckoning me to the seat that she had saved for me. "Is something up?

Where've you been? You're not sick or something, are you?"

"No," I whispered between my clenched teeth. "Course not." I got my geography stuff out of my bag.

"So why weren't you on the bus?" Anna asked. Obviously, Joey hadn't told her. So was I going to have to endure even more humiliation by telling her myself? It looked like I might avoid it for a bit longer, though, because at that moment, Mrs. Dalton walked in and the lesson began.

When the bell went for break at the end of the double lesson, Anna grabbed my arm and escorted me out of the room.

"What are you doing?" I hissed, trying to pull my elbow out of Anna's viselike grip.

"Taking you somewhere that you can tell me what's going on," Anna muttered back, and shoved our way through the throng of kids in the corridor like some kind of American footballer. Kids were pushed out of Anna's path as easily as gnats being swotted with one of those fly things. Splat, splat, splat—they all fell out of Anna's way. She didn't stop until we got right out of the building.

"Where are we going?" I protested, still trying to shrug off Anna's grip.

"To the library," she explained. "So that we can talk."

"The library?" Miss Mathias was going to think I was a complete anorak at this rate. "You can't talk in the library," I said weakly. But there was no point in trying to stop Anna when she was in one of these moods.

Up in the library, Anna gave Miss Mathias one of her most cute smiles. Miss Mathias beamed at me, seeming to be oblivious that I was being held hostage by Anna, who then headed across to the far side of the shelves to sit us down at a table tucked well back from most people's view.

"So," said Anna, pushing me into the chair next to the one she sat in. "What's up?"

"I told you—nothing." And I blinked, hoping that the tears I could feel at the back of my eyes were just so not going to happen.

"Pants on fire!" Anna exclaimed. "You weren't exactly that chatty yesterday, Beth. I tried to ring you when I got back from the Dungeon thing. But you didn't answer your phone. Or my text message. Or my e-mails."

It was true. After the gobstopper from Joey last night, I'd switched my phone off. And I hadn't bothered to switch on my PC, in a deliberate effort to avoid Anna for as long as possible. Anyway, I hadn't got the energy.

"So?"

"So what?" I asked. I just couldn't think of how to phrase the fact that her brother had dumped me by text message. The shame.

"So, for God's sake, what is wrong with you, Beth? Has your budgie died? Or your brother puked in your trainers? Or have you just been told that your eyebrows need plucking? Or has something more serious happened?"

I shrugged my shoulders and hung my head down. The fortunate thing about having grown my hair so much longer was that I could now hide behind my hair in situations like this.

"Hello?" Anna parted my hair with her hands and stuck her face right into mine, pulling her Shrek face as she did.

I couldn't help but laugh, despite myself.

"That's more like it. So—for the last time, tell me what's up or I will chop off your hair and tell Nicky to find a new model!"

"Anna! Don't you dare!"

"So come on, tell me what's up? Huge explosive row with your mum?"

"No!" I moaned.

"Murdered your brother?"

I just closed my eyes, wishing she'd go away and leave me to wallow in my misery.

"Or is it," Anna persisted, "something to do with Joey?"

"Oh, God," I moaned, putting my hands over my face and sinking down into the table as Anna pulled away. "He hasn't told you, has he?"

"*Der*—no! Would I need to ask you if I knew? What has Joey done? Farted in front of your dad? Or worse, your mum?"

I couldn't help laughing. "No—Joey didn't come home with me last night, did he?"

"So what, please, please, please, *please* tell me, has Joey done?" Anna said dramatically, beating her palms on the tabletop so loudly that Miss Mathias came over and asked us to keep the noise down. I'm sure that if more kids used the library in the first place, she'd probably have thrown us out, but it was nice to have the place looking busy.

"Sorry. Sure." Anna smiled at Miss Mathias and then turned back to me and raised her eyebrows expectantly.

"Oh, you might as well see this," I said, flicking my phone on and handing it to Anna. "It's the last message yesterday." I looked out of the window, not wanting to see Anna's face when she finally saw what I was on about. It seemed easier to show her than explaining it.

"Er, no," Anna replied, flicking through the phone menu. "The last message—the last two, actually—are from me."

"I mean the one from Joey," I muttered from my hand, which was cupped under my chin, my eyes low and avoiding her.

Anna fell silent as she went into the phone's memory and read what flashed up on the screen.

"You are joking! *He* is joking! He *never* did! And he did it *in a text*?" Anna looked at me, eyes agog.

So there it was. I was right—he had given me the push.

"He *dumped you* in a *text message*?"

"Anna!" I hissed, longing for her to be quieter. I didn't want anyone else to know about it. I certainly didn't want Frankie to find out—and you never knew where Frankie was lurking with her Ettes. She was always closer than the comfort zone for my liking.

"I hate him!" Anna said, grabbing my hand.

"You really didn't know?" I was a little bit surprised that Joey hadn't mentioned it to Anna, but maybe that was because he was hardly bothered about it. Ugh, my head was hurting again.

"No, I did not!" Anna exclaimed. "Do you think I wouldn't have been straight round to see you last night if I did? I tell you, I hate him!"

"But he's your brother, Anna," I sighed. "It's just hideous."

"No—*he's* hideous. He's a coward, and a moron. And I hate him."

"You can't hate him—he's your brother," I replied.

"Precisely," Anna said. "He's my brother—so that's another reason to hate him, isn't it?"

"And he's dumped me. I think he thought I was boring."

"Well, he's wrong—and he hardly gave you a chance, anyway," Anna explained. "I mean, you didn't see that much of him, did you? He's always at football, for a start. Plus he's always acting like some kid with Sam."

"But you're always laughing when they're larking about," I said. "You look like you think they're fun."

"In small doses they are, sure," Anna replied. "But who wants to be with someone like that all the time?"

"Don't you?" I asked. "I mean, isn't that what it's like with Sam when you're on your own?"

"Well, granted I spend more time with Sam than you do, er—did, with Joey. But we had serious chats too." Anna looked a bit distant for a few moments.

"But I don't want to be attached to him at the hip, for heaven's sake. I can't bear all that stuff you hear girls saying about their 'other halves.' Like there's only half of them? Or they are only half as interesting if they are on their own. No, thanks. I'm happy to be a whole person in my own right and spend time on my own and—more important—time with my best mate."

"So you're not cross with me?" I knew it was a weird question but I felt like I really needed to know the answer.

"Cross with you?" Anna queried. "Why should I be cross with you? You're my best mate."

"Your best mate who got dumped by your brother," I pointed out. "So it's going to be tricky, isn't it?"

"Is it?" Anna looked puzzled. "Why?"

"Every time I go round to yours," I stated. "And Joey's there."

"Not embarrassing for me, it's not," Anna said. "Or for you, either!"

"But it *is*!" I wailed, dragging my fingers through my hair in despair.

"Embarrassing for Joey, maybe," Anna exclaimed. "But certainly not for you, Beth! Oh, no! It will not be remotely embarrassing for you! *He's* the dork! *Joey's* the moron. You are just the one who's been hurt."

"The victim," I sighed.

"Victim? Excuse me? Did I hear you right?" Anna put her hand to her ear like she was deaf. "Victim you are not! You, Beth, are the girl that Joey is very much going to regret he let get away. . . ."

"Oh, sure," I said. "NOT!"

"Oh, he will," Anna said, her determined face even more determined than ever. "You mark my words," Anna carried on. "Joey is going to live to regret dumping you in a text message. In fact, he's going to regret dumping you FULL STOP!"

And that was when Miss Mathias *did* decide that she was going to have to kick us out.

Chapter Ten
Could You Live Without a Boy?

And so the day went on. I have to admit that after I'd done my homework that evening, I did switch my phone back on. If I'm honest, it was because I wanted to see if Joey had suddenly changed his mind and had sent me a text saying that he thought I was really cool and funny and good fun.

But of course he hadn't. I'd switched my phone back off in disgust and wallowed in feeling sorry for myself.

I thought a bit more about what Anna had said about making Joey regret dumping me. Somehow, I couldn't see why he would. I mean, I couldn't just suddenly have a personality transplant, could I? Suddenly turn into some kind of cheerleader who was always the life and soul of one of Joey's stupid pranks. Okay, so I'm not the sort of person who wants to be the center of attention all the time. But then, I don't think I'm that boring, either. After all, Anna's always a good laugh and she doesn't seem to think I'm from Dullsville.

Maybe I just had to accept the fact that I'm not the right person for this boyfriend/girlfriend thing. . . .

"Well, hi, Beth! Great earrings!"

I was standing washing my hands in the senior girls' loos and was actually in the process of taking the earrings out. They were one of my best pairs and I wouldn't normally wear them to school, but this thing with Joey had really bothered me. I thought that if I started being a bit jazzier in my appearance, maybe I'd be a bit jazzier in my personality. But I'd only had them in until break time before Mrs. Stokes, my English teacher, had spotted them and told me to take them out. So much for being cool, then. And now Frankie was moving in on me. What did she want?

"So how are you, then, Beth?" Frankie drooled on.

Like she cared? Like she really wanted to know. What did she want?

"Er, fine, thanks," I spluttered, popping the earrings into my pocket and moving over to the dryer.

"Only you look a bit down," Frankie went on.

"Sorry?"

"Doesn't she, girls?" Frankie enquired of the Franki-ettes, who all nodded like one of those kitsch dogs you see in the back shelf of cars. "Is there anything we can help with?"

What was she on about? "No—I'm fine, thanks. Excuse me, I'd better go and find Anna." I tried to make my exit but Frankie and the Ettes immediately moved and formed a kind of semicircle in front of me. "I said I need to go and find Anna."

"Oh, she'll be somewhere outside," Frankie said. "But hey, Beth. So sorry to hear about your boyfriend."

I felt my face flush instantly. "What?"

"Your boyfriend. I gather you've split up? Omigod, it must be *so* horrid for you. *So* ghastly. I hope you were the one who got in first? You know—dumped him?"

"Excuse me—I have to go," I said, struggling through.

But Frankie wasn't going to give up easily. She never had, so I shouldn't really have been surprised.

"Only I heard about it from Anna," Frankie niggled on. "She was saying that Joey was the one that gave you the sack. Dreadful. At least, I assume it must be. Of course I've never been dumped myself. But—hey, boys, eh?"

The Franki-ettes whimpered, apparently sympathetically—but somehow, I didn't think they were that sad for me.

But Anna? *Anna* had told them about Joey? How could she? But they couldn't have heard from anyone else as Joey was the only other person who knew.

Storming out of the loos, I steamed to the vending machines, where I found Anna retrieving a bottle of water from the tray at the bottom.

"I think you and I need to talk!" I fumed, hooking Anna out into the courtyard.

"What's up?" she spluttered. "It's not my fault Mrs. Stokes saw your earrings!"

"This is nothing to do with earrings!" I ranted on. "I've just seen darling Frankie in the loos. How come you told her about Joey and me?"

"Joey and you?" Anna looked incredulous. "What do you mean? Why would I have told Frankie about it? As if!"

"Well, she says you did!" I raged. "And if you didn't tell her, how on earth would she know about it? Nobody else knows."

"Beth, give me a break! Do you honestly think that I would go and talk to Frankie about anything under normal circumstances, let alone talk to her about something involving my best mate?"

134

I looked at Anna and didn't know what to say. Because what she was saying to me was so right. So not what would have happened.

"So how does Frankie know about Joey, then? How does she even know that we've split up—let alone that he was the one who split with me?"

Anna shrugged her shoulders. "How would I know what that witch-in-training is capable of?"

I angrily took a kick at an innocent weed that was growing peacefully up through a crack in the court-yard paving.

"Oh . . ." Anna exhaled. "Oh, woah. Jeez. I think I've worked it out. . . ."

"What? Tell me?"

"She must have heard me on the phone yesterday. After I left you when I got off the bus yesterday after-noon. I called Joey on my way home and told him what I thought of him and his scummy behavior. The only thing I can think is that Frankie must have heard me on the phone to him. . . ." Now it was Anna's turn to blush with embarrassment. "I remem-ber now. I saw Frankie and her ducklings outside the newsagent just after I put the phone down on Joey . . . Oh, Beth! I am *so* sorry! It *was* me! She must have listened to me and then she pounced on you!"

"Anna!" I wailed. "Frankie—of all people!"

"But it's not like I did it on purpose, is it?"

I looked at Anna, who was as upset about it as I was. I knew it was true. Anna would never have split on me.

"Oh, don't worry about it," I said just as the bell went. "Come on—forget it. I just hope Frankie does too."

"Yeah," Anna said almost silently. "I suppose there's a fair chance she will, Beth. There'll soon be some other victim she can sink her teeth into about something, won't there?"

"I'm sorry to sound mean, but I do hope so," I replied.

For obvious reasons, I avoided going back to Anna's house after school all that week. I just didn't know how I could face Joey at the moment. I mean, I realized that I couldn't avoid Anna's house forever and was bound to bump into Joey at some stage. But just not now, thanks.

On Friday evening, Anna and I both turned up at the Cutting Room for another practice session with Nicky. It was just what I needed and I felt like a complete princess being preened and pampered. Nicky had even arranged for the woman who ran the coolest of cool clothes shops in town to come along to select outfits for the three of us models to wear.

The woman, whose name was Cherca (she was dead tall and dead glamorous), picked out stuff for all of us to wear. She even found things for Nicky and Anna, and all the other Cutting Room staff, that suited their black-only uniform. We all looked great. And with my hair tressed up, I felt great too.

The competition was going to be the next weekend at a hotel in central London. Nicky told us all that we needed to be at the salon at some unearthly hour on the Sunday morning. We'd be taken to the hotel in a minibus, spend the day at the hotel doing the competition, and then return home after the prize-giving at the end of the day.

"You looked dead cool," Anna said in her mum's car on our way home. (I noticed that Joey didn't suggest that he come to meet Anna that night. . . .)

"Thanks," I replied. "You looked great too."

"Nicky says he'll blow-dry my hair for me on the Sunday morning if I turn up with it wet," Anna explained.

"Cool."

"Yeah—but think how early I'm going to have to get into the shower! Yuck!"

I laughed in commiseration.

"So, what are you doing tomorrow night after work?" Anna wanted to know.

I hadn't even thought about it. "Dunno."

"Fancy coming to the cinema?"

"What's on?" I asked.

"That new superscary film about the kids who go away for the weekend. You know, the one they keep advertising on the telly where they turn up at their gran's but the house is empty? Spooooky!"

"Oh yeah—I know the one. Yeah—maybe," I agreed.

"Great." Anna grinned. "We can grab something to eat after work and go to the early evening showing."

The cinema turned out to be a moment of mega-embarrassment. Because of course Sam was going to see the movie with Anna, wasn't he? And he was okay-ish about it when he realized that I was going too. But it was obvious that he didn't really want me there once the film was over.

So, despite Anna making noises about me coming over to the NafCaf with them afterward for an ice cream (which under any other circumstances I would have been front of the queue for), I hopped on a bus and came home on my own. My mum would have died if she'd known—she's convinced that People Who Do Horrible Things don't do them to people who aren't on their own.

So I lied to Mum when I got home and said that

Sam and Anna had walked me to the door before they'd gone on to Anna's. Mum bought it and, in my guilt, I sucked up and made her and Dad some coffee before I went to bed.

Actually, Mum had been quite normal with me about the Joey thing. I think she'd kind of realized quite quickly that things with Joey weren't happening anymore. But she didn't go on about it and get all soppy with me. She just sort of let me know that she knew without telling me. Cool.

"Beth, I really do need your help with this history stuff!" Anna pleaded with me on Thursday as we made our way home from the bus stop. "Please say you'll come back and help me with it. Please, please! I can feed you one of Mum's double chocolate chip muffins she made the other day."

"Oh yeah? As if there are any left!" I laughed. If it had been me and Jack, I doubt very much if there would have been any.

"Well, I think there will be," Anna said, clearly not sure herself. "Anyway—come and help me with history?"

I wasn't sure. The muffin was tempting, I admit. But I wasn't sure that I wanted to run the risk of seeing Joey.

"Tell you what," I offered. "Why don't I help you at the weekend? You could make some more muffins with your mum and come and bring some over to mine so we can scoff and work."

"Small problem of no time at the weekend, Beth!" Anna stated. "We've got work on Saturday and the hair competition on the Sunday, remember?"

"Of course!" I said.

"So you'll come back with me now, then?" Anna asked, dragging me down the side street that led to her road.

It looked like I had no choice. Fortunately, the house was empty when we arrived. Unfortunately, so was the muffin tin. But we managed to find some chocolate biscuits, which we took with us up to Anna's room, where we spent an hour sorting out Anna's problem with her coursework. I love history but Anna's not that fussed about it. It's not that she's too dumb to do her homework—it was really because she just wasn't interested in it.

"Look." I glanced at my watch. "I've got to go or Mum will give me a hard time for leaving Jack on his own for so long."

I shoved all my stuff back into my bag and started to stomp down the stairs. Anna came down to see me out.

"Anna?"

Bummer. Joey appeared out of the kitchen and into the hallway. He must have gotten back while we were upstairs and we hadn't heard him over the noise of Anna's CD.

"Oh, it's you." Joey froze in his tracks, just as surprised as I was.

"Hi," I said. It seemed pretty lame, but I didn't know what else I was meant to say to a former boyfriend. I suppose, if I'd had time to think about it, "Let me stick my fingers in your eyes" would have been more what I'd felt like saying. But I don't think that quickly. Not in circumstances like that.

"You okay?" Joey asked. Like he really wanted to know? I doubted it.

"Sure." I carried on down the stairs, hoping that my cheeks weren't that flushed. But again I doubted it. "See you tomorrow," I said to Anna over my shoulder.

"Yeah," she replied. "Bye!"

I was out of that door and off down the road faster than I have ever walked in my life. But even before I could get home, my phone went beep.

It was a text from Anna. God Ur COl!

In a weird way, I was glad that I'd got the First Meeting After Being Dumped with Joey out of the way. Now it had happened, I didn't have to worry about it going to happen. So I could get on with still trying to work out what I'd done wrong.

I didn't talk about it much with Anna, but when I did, she just kept on saying that it wasn't my problem, it was Joey's problem. Anna also pointed out that Joey had never managed to keep a girlfriend longer than a few weeks. I know she thought that might make me feel better. But honestly, you know it didn't help much to know that I was just one in a long line of girls. I was just grateful that Joey didn't go to my school and I didn't have to try to avoid him on a daily basis.

Strangely, after the incident in the loo, it was dead easy to avoid Frankie at school. I think she went off the idea of bothering with me when she realized that she wasn't going to make me burst into tears. Anyway, like Anna had suggested, she moved on to some other sucker in Year Nine who she'd heard had been to do an audition for the next Harry Potter movie. It seemed like the poor kid was in grave danger of becoming a Franki-ette. Hopefully, she'd be saved and realize before it was too late. . . .

"Morning," Anna groaned dramatically as she clutched her head.

Anyone else would have assumed that Anna was

tired from hanging out the night before. I, of course, knew it was because she'd had to get up at five that morning in order to be at the Cutting Room to get everything ready for the competition. I thought Anna was pretty cool to do it. Normally, for anything else, I can't imagine that Anna would have been bothered to get up. She'd have to have about six alarm clocks go off, and then still be thrown out of bed by her mum.

So I could tell by the fact that she was ready to go so early that Anna was really enjoying working with Nicky and the other people at the Cutting Room. Even if she was still moaning about it being early.

"Okay, okay," Nicky said, bustling around the salon. "Hi, Beth—thanks for turning up so early!"

"Oh, thanks a bunch! You never thanked me!" Anna wailed.

"That's because you're being paid to be here early!" Nicky barked, winking conspiratorially at me. "So get on with things. Have we got the bag with the shampoos and treatments?"

"Yes," Anna replied, pointing to it. "And the hair-spray, the scissors, the towels, the mirrors ... everything." Anna finished showing Nicky where each bag or container was.

"Right, then, if everything is ready and everyone

is here," Nicky spun round on his heel, "then we'd better get going."

We all bundled into the minibus and cheered with appreciation as Shaz, one of the other stylists, immediately proffered a bag of pastries and a selection of drinks from a bright pink picnic box.

"Don't drink too much or we'll have to stop so that you can go to the loo," Nicky lectured.

"Oooooooo!" we chorused back sarcastically.

"What?" Nicky said in mock offense. "I was only saying."

"Saying that he was dead nervous, more like," Anna whispered to me.

I knew she was right and smiled back to her.

As everyone was settled, the bus driver indicated to pull off.

"Wait!" Nicky screamed.

"What now?" asked Shaz.

"Sorry," Nicky spluttered, opening the door of the bus again. "I've forgotten the camera. . . ."

The competition was just fab. Fab, fab, fab! I loved everything about it. Actually, it was a huge event. Anna and I hadn't realized until we got there that there would be so many people in the competition.

The place was a buzz of activity and Nicky got even more nervous when we arrived. In fact, so nervous that his face went green and we all thought he was going to puke. Fortunately, he didn't. But he did go into megabossy mode and started bossing us all around: "You sit here! You wash her hair! You— where's my scissors?"

Amazingly, no one fell out with him. Everyone just got on with whatever job they had to do and things pretty much went according to the plan that Nicky and Shaz had obviously agreed on beforehand.

Anna was amazing. Dead cool. It was like she'd always spent Sunday mornings taking part in major hairdressing competitions in London. She just got on with helping Nicky out, almost like those people you see in operating rooms on the telly. You know, the ones who hand over the scissors and suction tubes to the surgeons? That was Anna! That was how sorted she was.

Meanwhile, I had to sit down and . . . just *sit*, really. Chloe, the makeup girl who did the nails at the salon, came over to do my face. It looked amazing. Truly amazing! I tried to concentrate on what it was she did with eye shadow and mascara to make my eyes look ten times bigger than they did when I put makeup on. My lips were big and glossy and . . . gorgeous!

Then Nicky turned to me and my hair was tweaked and sprayed and perfected. There was not a fizz of a frizzy bit in sight as the hair irons pulled my hair down over one side of my face and looked double the length that it had been such a short time ago.

"Wow, Beth!" Anna said, beaming from ear to ear in appreciation as she came over to my mirror when Nicky had finished.

"Isn't she fantastic?" Nicky smiled, looking dead pleased with himself. "I've got to have a photo of this! But, Beth, just don't move a muscle! You have to stay completely still until the judging!"

Actually, sitting still for so long was agonizing. I wanted to look around the place, check out the styles the other salons were doing. But I wasn't allowed to. And I was starving—but Nicky wouldn't let me eat either. He said I might mess up my hair and makeup and there wasn't any time to touch anything up. Great. Good thing I didn't need the loo.

The judging itself was quite bizarre. The three of us who had been styled by Nicky and Shaz had to sit in the middle of a kind of central podium. We were surrounded by all the other "hairstyles," sitting under these blazing hot lights. I'd been given strict instructions by Nicky not to smile.

Instead, he told me to pout like a kid sulking because their big brother had just broken their Barbie. I did my best, but I have to say I felt a bit of a twit. I just told myself to imagine that all the other models were doing the same thing—if only I could be given permission to see.

The judges said zilch. They just came around, said nothing to us, but either walked around us, checking out the hair from all angles, or made notes on their clipboards.

Even when the judging was all over, Nicky wouldn't let any of us eat anything—in case we spilled stuff down our clothes—although he did, finally, let us sip some water through a straw. The tension was dreadful. Even Anna seemed twitchy. I had butterflies in my stomach as if I was about to take an exam that I hadn't studied for. Even though it wasn't up to me to win! I couldn't bear it.

"Uh-oh—I think this is it!" Nicky hissed when he spotted the team of judges climb up onto the podium.

"Ladies and gentlemen," said the judge who was obviously in charge. She'd certainly been the one who led the way with the others trooping behind her when they were checking us out. "I am delighted to announce the winners of this year's Clip and Snip competition. . . ."

❧

"What a result!" Nicky said as we all bundled back into the minibus, tired and exhausted at the end of the day. "Well done, everyone! You've all been great!"

"Yeah!" we all agreed, and sank back into our seats.

"So how does it feel to have been one of the models for an award-winning stylist?" Anna squeezed my hand and grinned.

"Mega." I beamed. "So how does it feel to work for him?"

"Mega mega!" Anna confirmed. "Three cheers for Nicky and Shaz!"

Everyone on the bus cheered back.

"So how does it feel to be Best Newcomers?" I asked Nicky.

"Like all my birthdays have come at once." Nicky beamed. "Christmases, too! You know, Beth—you can have a free style every week if you'll agree to come along next year!"

"Cheers, Nicky!" I smiled at Anna. "How fab is that?"

"'Cos next year, everyone," Nicky continued, "we're going to go for Salon of the Year!"

Chapter Eleven
What Kind of Girl Are You?

"*Quick! She's coming!*" Anna hissed, and spread the local newspaper out on the table before her.

"Anna!" I protested, admittedly weakly.

We were sitting in the crowded lunch hall, hogging the last table. Anna had somehow managed to persuade everyone that we were saving the seats for someone. It was not true. Except, I suppose, we *were* saving the seats—for Frankie and the Frankiettes.

Admittedly, this was not a normal situation. But Anna had an ulterior motive.

Frankie sauntered along the lines of chairs, getting closer to us, eyes sweeping to and fro as she scouted for a free table. She and her cohorts had to admit defeat when she got up to ours.

"Anna, Beth," said one of Frankie's henchmen curtly. "Um, there doesn't appear to be anyone sitting here?"

"Oh, you mean you want to sit down here?" Anna said innocently. "Sure, let me just move this paper. Sorry, we were just looking at Beth's photo!"

Anna folded the newspaper in her usual dramatic fashion.

"Excuse me?" Frankie said, stepping forward and her cohorts slipping to one side like she was the royalty they clearly thought she was. "Did you say Beth's photo was in the paper?"

"Oh—haven't you seen it?" Anna smiled sweetly, not glancing in my direction at all.

I would have been more than happy for Frankie never to have seen the photo. Don't get me wrong, I was really pleased with it. I just didn't need a winding-up session with Frankie.

"Doesn't she look fab?" Anna lathered it on thick.

I had to admit that I loved that photo. It was the one that Nicky had taken of me at the show—and now it was in the local paper!

"Excuse me?" Clearly, Frankie couldn't believe that I was in the paper. "What is this?"

Frankie let out a little gasp as she leaned forward and saw my photo.

If I say so myself, I looked stunning. And Frankie just couldn't handle it.

"You won a prize?" she said, her voice rising in horror.

"Well," I spluttered. "It wasn't actually me that won the prize—"

"But she was the model!" Anna finished the sentence for me.

"You? A model?" Frankie gaped at me in disbelief. The Ettes were looking equally worried.

I ran my fingers through my silken hair, which was still glowing from the treatments that Nicky had sent me home with after the show.

"She's the top house model at the salon." Anna rubbed it in a bit more for good measure. "Anyway, we'd best go, Frankie. People to see, places to go. Ciao!"

Anna took the paper from Frankie and started to leave the dining hall. Standing up, I grabbed my bag and Anna's, which she'd left behind in her exit flourish, and zipped off to catch her up.

"What's with the Italian?" I asked, coming up to her.

"Who knows?" Anna giggled. "But I just loved every minute of rubbing Frankie's nose in it."

"So did I!" I laughed.

We stopped off at the corner shop on our way home that afternoon and collected the latest copy of *Get It!* Still basking in the glory of our weekend of success, we went back to Anna's house to chill out.

"Disgusting trousers!" Anna exclaimed as we sat in her room and she flicked through her copy.

"Quiz!" Anna said, sitting up sharply and reaching for a pen from her bag.

"Oh, do we have to?" I whined, thinking back to the last quiz that had caused me so much angst.

"Of course we do," retorted Anna. "Come on, Beth!"

"Okay, okay," I murmured. "What is it this time?"

"What Kind of Girl Are You?" Anna said with relish. "Now, question one . . ."

So half an hour later, questions answered, Anna was acting as judge and jury.

"So," Anna stated in her best Natasha Kaplinksy telly voice. "Beth Clarkson: What Kind of Girl Are You?" She did a mock drumroll and totted up my score. "Beth Clarkson: 'You obviously get stressed about things. Lighten up! The world won't end if you don't have a boyfriend.'"

"I don't believe it says that!" I interrupted and grabbed the magazine from Anna, scanning down the page. To my amazement, it did indeed say that!

"If I could just continue." Anna snatched the magazine back and searched down to find her place again. "Okay . . . 'You are full of life and talent, girl! Relax— you are a star already. Just don't worry so much!' You see," Anna pointed out. "What did I tell you?"

"Okay," I said. "So what about you? What does it say about you?"

Anna scanned down the page and worked out her score before she carried on. "Right . . . 'You know what you want and you know how to get it.'" I couldn't help laughing out loud at that one. Spot on.

"Excuse me," Anna said, pretending to be insulted. "If you'd just let me finish. . . . 'But sometimes you should back off on the full impact. You can, just sometimes, be a bit bossy.'"

Now I really was laughing.

"Well, really!" Anna said, and threw her cushion at me, laughing as well.

Suddenly there was a knock at Anna's door.

"Anna?" Without waiting for an answer, the caller opened up and walked in.

"Oh no . . . erm . . . sorry."

It was Joey. And he was carrying the local paper. I wanted the world to swallow me up.

"Yes?" Anna said. "You want something, Joey?"

Joey blushed. "Yes . . . no . . . Hi, Beth . . . erm, forget it."

"So you've seen the paper, then?" Anna had no intention of forgetting it. "Have you seen Beth's photo?"

"Oh, that . . . ," he said, blushing some more. "Urm, yeah, I suppose I had."

"Looks fantastic, doesn't she?" Anna went.

"Anna!" I hissed. This was too embarrassing for words.

"Yes, she does," Joey agreed. "Your hair looks really nice, Beth."

He stood there, making us all embarrassed, and then Anna said, "If that's all you came to tell us, then you can go. Bye, Joey!"

"Sure." Joey turned to leave. "See you, Beth."

"Sure," I said.

He closed the door behind him.

"Ha!" Anna said, tossing the magazine down on the floor. "Told you!"

"Told me what?" I asked.

"That he was going to regret what he did!"

"Nah . . . ," I said. "But do you think he has?"

"Of course!" Anna said. "But listen—you've got to do what the quiz said." She picked up the magazine again and flicked back to the quiz page. "'The world won't end if you don't have a boyfriend. You are full of life and talent, girl! Relax—you are a star already. Just don't worry so much!'"

"Okay, then," I laughed. "I'll do my best. But quizzes are so boring. I just don't want to know about what should and shouldn't happen in my life. I just want to get on and see what happens."

"Too right," agreed Anna. "Be chilled."

We sat in silence for a second, looking at the beauty pages and pondering on the latest must-have mascaras.

"Tell you what, though," I said.

"What?"

"Where's the horoscope page? Let's see what they say."

"Beth! Horoscopes? You *are* kidding!"

About the Author

Caroline Plaisted worked in publishing for fourteen years before becoming a full-time writer. She has written for the BBC, Bloomsbury, and Kingfisher. She lives in Ashford near Kent with her two children, two dogs, and two cats.